PARANORMAL UNIVERSITY: FOURTH SEMESTER

PARANORMAL UNIVERSITY: FOURTH SEMESTER

PARANORMAL UNIVERSITY™ BOOK FOUR

JACE MITCHELL

MICHAEL ANDERLE

DISRUPTIVE IMAGINATION

LMBPN Publishing
PMB 196, 2540 South Maryland Pkwy
Las Vegas, NV 89109

First US edition, May 2020
Version 1.01, February 2021
eBook ISBN: 978-1-64202-932-1
Print ISBN: 978-1-64202-933-8

Thanks to the JIT Readers

Misty Roa
Jackey Hankard-Brodie
Diane L. Smith
Kerry Mortimer
Veronica Stephan-Miller
Debi Sateren

If I've missed anyone, please let me know!

Editor
SkyHunter Editing Team

For Maître d's everywhere.

— Jace

*To Family, Friends and
Those Who Love
to Read.
May We All Enjoy Grace
to Live the Life We Are
Called.*

— Michael

The five looked up at the mountain, their petty differences suddenly disappearing as if they'd never existed. The small arguments no longer mattered. How could they in the face of such...wonder?

The fat man named Fred laughed, his belly shaking so hard that his shirt rose. His pale, hairy skin was ignored by all. Even his laugh was ignored.

Andrew's suit was impeccable, as always. "I know. I know," he whispered to an invisible creature only he could see. He didn't pull his eyes away from the mountain.

It floated hundreds of yards above and in front of them. It was massive on the scale of multiple European cathedrals, spanning miles of sky.

Bill had thick glasses and a habit of swearing most people thought was outrageous, but he couldn't tame it. "How the fuck are we supposed to get up there?"

No one said anything, because no one was sure. The five staring at the floating mountain had thought this day would come...but not really. It was far too good to be true.

They stood at the edge of a thick forest, with trees that stretched a hundred feet tall, and in front of them was a beach that ran into a rolling ocean. The waves crashed against the sand, louder and larger than most people on Earth had ever seen.

But they weren't on Earth. No one on that planet would believe them, at least not for a few years, but these five had passed through a barrier they called the Veil. They were staring at Mount Olympus, hanging above Poseidon's domain.

A long path had led these five here, but it wasn't one they thought about now. No, as they looked at the massive rock floating like a balloon, they could only think about moving forward. Or rather, up.

Andrew shoved his hands into his pockets. He couldn't stop staring at the hovering mountain. "She wants to know the same thing. How do we get up there?"

The thin women at the edge of the group were identical twins. They were short, under five feet tall, and very homely. They clearly had no answer to the question.

The fat man, Fred, finally turned around and looked at the forest. "Someone has to come get us. I mean, someone brought us here, right? There's no way they'd just leave us on this beach staring upward."

As if someone were listening, a cloud started floating down toward them.

Andrew shook his head. "She doesn't like that. She doesn't like it one bit."

No one else said anything, only stared in amazement as the cloud descended from the heavens. Their eyes grew wider until each of them looked like their eyeballs might pop out of their faces and roll into the ocean.

The cloud stopped before them, hovering over the beach as waves gently lapped the sand.

Bill, the one with the Coke-bottle glasses, took a step back. "What in the fuck of all fuckery is this?"

One of the twins, Octavia, stepped forward with her hand outstretched. Her fingers moved through the cloud, encountering nothing of substance to stop it. "It's no magic carpet."

Without taking his eyes from the new arrival, Bill said, "It certainly isn't going to hold fat man Fred. The whole thing will collapse."

Fred chuckled. "Watch this, Billy-boy." He moved to the cloud, his wide berth forcing Octavia to take a step back, and shoved both hands deep into the mist. He was too large to simply hop up on it, but he got one leg over the edge and then pulled himself up. He turned around, lying on the cloud, his large stomach heaving. "See, Billy-boy? If you can believe it, you can achieve it."

Everyone else was staring with slack jaws.

Fred lifted a chunk of cloud, pulling it apart like it was cotton candy. He tossed it at the group. "This thing will hold us, so get on before it leaves. Isn't this why we crossed over? So that we could see stuff like this?"

The twins looked at one another while Andrew looked at his invisible—or imaginary—friend.

The foul-mouthed Bill said, "Fuck it." He went forward, and although he was shorter than Fred, he managed to scamper onto the cloud. He hopped up on his feet, the cloud rising midway to his shin. He stared down, speechless.

The twins shrugged and climbed up, then lay on their backs and stared at the sky. "It's like lying on the softest bed ever," Jess said as her fingers caressed the mist.

Andrew was still standing on the beach. "She doesn't want to get up there."

The cloud floated around Bill like white smoke as he stared at his feet. "Someone tell that shit-for-brains jackass to get up here. He just crossed worlds, but now he won't get on a damned cloud."

Octavia flipped over so she was lying on her stomach and looked at Andrew. "You and she better get up here. It might take off on its own."

He shook his head, obviously not pleased, but there weren't many other places he could go. Truthfully, they hadn't crossed the Veil on their own but had been pulled across. By what? They weren't sure, but they wanted to be here. They'd been searching for this for years, and they'd finally found it.

Andrew took a step back and then ran forward, his athletic legs propelling him up onto the cloud. Once there, he turned around and offered his hand to the being no one else had ever seen. Indeed, the other four doubted it existed.

Once all five plus the imaginary friend were on the cloud, it flew into the sky. The five scurried to the sides. They peered at the ocean and beach below, not quite believing this was happening.

"We're actually here," Jess whispered. "All this time, and we're finally being brought to the source."

The cloud continued its ascent, the air growing colder around them the higher they went.

"They should have put a heater on this damned thing," Bill cursed. His voice didn't hold any anger, only wonder at what was now a few feet away.

The mountain soared in front of them. Huge mansions were carved into the cliff faces, buildings with spiral towers that looked like they might touch heaven. Smaller clouds floated around the peaks, and birds flew around it. From here, the mountain looked as big as the world beneath them.

The cloud reached the edge of the floating fortress and stopped. A foot of open air separated them from a flat sandy landing.

Fred laughed heartily. "If they think I'm going to risk hauling my fat ass across that space, they've grossly overestimated my manhood. You all go on up there and tell me what you find. I'll be waiting right here."

Thunder rolled across the sky the moment he finished his sentence.

Octavia's head turned to the mountain's top. "Someone's not happy about that, Fred. Better make the jump."

Andrew wasted no time. He simply hopped across, landing easily on the mountain. He didn't wait for those behind him but started following the sandy trail that led upward.

Bill frowned. "I'll be damned if that suit-wearing sissy makes it up there before me." He didn't look at anyone else, but using his short, powerful legs, catapulted himself across the space and onto the floating mountain.

Octavia smiled and looked at her sister. "You first."

Jess rolled her eyes but looked confident enough. She made the jump easily and had barely landed when Octavia touched down next to her. They looked at Fred. "You really going to stay there?" Jess asked.

Fred wasn't laughing anymore, but rather growing pale. He was staring at the open air separating him from the mountain, obviously thinking there was no way he could make it.

"You can do it," Octavia told him.

Fred shook his head, closed his eyes, and took a deep breath. When he let the breath out, he started running, eyes opening a second before he leaped.

The ladies moved quickly, parting to let the huge man crash onto the sandy landing. Fred rolled over onto his back and started laughing. "First time any of you seen a pig fly," he said between gulps of air and laughter.

Octavia looked up the path. "Come on, big man. They're leaving us behind."

Fred rolled onto his stomach and then pushed himself to his feet. The three followed their compatriots, heading into a world of magic none of them understood.

The five followed the trail as it wound around the mountain, slowly going higher.

Bill commented at one point, "This is like Mario 64," although when the others asked what he meant, he refused to answer. The air grew colder, until each of them thought they'd surely have to turn back around or freeze to death. Eventually, though, they found themselves in front of huge iron doors that stood fifteen feet high. Lightning-bolt insignias were engraved on each, and the handle on each door was the same bolt.

The iron doors guarded one of the mansions they had seen while flying here, and it was the first one they'd come to on this trail.

Andrew looked at the windows lining the building. It was impossible to see through any of them. "It can't be him, can it?"

Bill stepped up to the door on the right side. "Who the fuck else do you think lives in the clouds with lightning bolts decorating their doors? Your mom?"

Bill didn't consult anyone about what happened next. He raised his hand, made a fist, and banged three times on the door.

Long moments passed, Bill frowning when nothing responded to his knock. He raised his hand once more, but before he could bang again, the door opened with a loud creak.

It moved inward slowly, revealing a foyer unlike any the five had ever seen. Statues that looked like Greek gods lined the walls and stood upon a marble floor. The twins' eyes grew wide as they stared, and none of the five moved. They were more afraid than when the cloud showed up to deliver them to the mountain.

A small man came around the door. He was wearing what looked like black spandex, which covered every part of his body except his head and hands. On his head, he wore a dunce cap.

Bill was short, but this man was *much* shorter. "Who in the hell are you?"

The little man spoke, and his voice was unexpected. From the size of him, a tiny, scratchy voice surely lived inside, but instead deep, commanding words came forth. "My name is Hermes, and we've been expecting you."

Fred smiled. "Hermes? Aren't you supposed to look more like the statues over there and less like Bill here?"

The small man's face grew stern. "If you *must* know, I angered Zeus a few days ago. This ridiculous body and outfit are my punishment. Hopefully he gets over it soon, because looking like *this* is perhaps the greatest wound I could be dealt. Come on, Zeus is waiting."

With that, the small man started into the mansion. He didn't so much as glance back to make sure they were following.

The five looked at each other, although no one said anything. Fred shrugged and was the first to step inside the house. The others came right after.

The Veil would begin tearing very, very soon.

CHAPTER ONE

Frank held a can of beer in his right hand. To Claire, it looked like some kind of fancy microbrew. "Lass, how are things going?"

"It's... It's different now." Claire looked at the skyscrapers around her. No matter how many times she came to downtown Boston, she never got used to them. It was so much different from the place she came from.

Frank zipped his jacket up. "It's damned cold here, and it's only September."

The leprechaun had disappeared after they returned from the battle with Hades. *He's almost like a cat*, Claire thought. The summer semester had ended and the fall one began without a word from him. Then this Saturday morning, he'd simply appeared in her new dorm room and said they should go get breakfast.

"How are things different?" he asked. "Or are you going to keep your dear friend Frank in suspense?"

"Well, for starters, Jack, Marissa, and I are no longer together."

Frank turned toward her, one eyebrow raised. "The band broke up?"

Claire grinned. She missed her friends. She missed being around them on a day to day basis. She missed how much Marissa worried, and she missed how much crap Jack talked. Frank was right, it did feel like they'd broken up the band. "Yeah, I guess so. A lot has changed. They decided we aren't supposed to be assassins but students, and for the second year of school, they've put us in 'tracks.' Jack, Marissa, and I are in different tracks."

Frank shook his head. "*Tracks*. What does that even mean? What track is Jack on, Professional Seduction Artist?"

Claire snorted. "He wishes. He's field operations, which means he *will* be an assassin when it's all said and done. They've got him lifting weights every day, and he's put on ten pounds since the last time you saw him. It hasn't done *anything* to help his ego."

Frank pointed with his free hand. "That place over there has good French toast. Want to do that?"

Claire shrugged. "Sure, sounds good."

Frank tilted his beer up and drained it, then gave a pretty strong belch before they started across the street. He tossed the can in a trash bin before entering the restaurant. They ordered food and drinks quickly, with the waitress giving Frank only the slightest of stares. It was like she could *nearly* see what he was, but not quite.

Frank placed both hands on the table. "Spill the beans. What track is Marissa in?"

Claire placed her hands in her lap and grinned. "Guess."

"Me gods," Frank blurted. "I haven't seen ye in months, and this is the treatment I get? Guessing games?"

Claire rolled her eyes before taking a sip of water. "You're no fun. Her track is experimental, actually. They're calling it Powers and Abilities."

Frank tapped his thumb on the table for a moment. "Is that like what those asswipes were able to do?"

Claire nodded. She stirred her water with her straw for a moment. "I'm a lot less in the loop these days because the FBI isn't asking us to go kill Mythers, but I don't think they have any idea why those people had powers. That's what they're using Marissa for. That and because she's the only one who can cast a spell."

Frank glanced around the room longingly. "I wish they served beer here. It's the only thing that's bad about this place. I should have just brought some in a flask." He sighed and put his eyes back on Claire. "Is that why you have that swanky dorm room all to yourself?"

Claire gave a half-frown. "Yeah. I wish Marissa was in it with me."

Frank pointed a stubby finger at her. "And what about ye? Where did you land in these tracks?"

Claire groaned. "I don't want to tell you."

"But tell me ye will," Frank retorted. "Let me hear it, lass."

Claire put her head in her hands and looked at the table. "Intelligence."

Frank giggled but quickly caught himself. "Sorry, lass, ye mumbled there. Mind saying it one more time?"

Claire sighed and pulled her head out of her hands, meeting Frank's eyes. "Intelligence."

Frank's eyes widened in mock surprise, his mouth opening as well. When he spoke, his voice was a fearful whisper. "We're doomed, lass. Doomed, I tell ye."

"Shut it, Frank," Claire said, rolling her eyes.

The leprechaun's head fell forward, smacking loudly onto the table. He brought his hands to his thick black hair and started pulling on it. "Zeus, save me. They've made the girl a part of intelligence. How have things ever gotten so bad? Why, oh, why did I not stick around and talk sense into these humans?"

Claire took hold of her water glass. "If you don't hush, Frank, you're going to be wearing my ice water."

Frank pulled his head off the table, a huge grin draped across his face. "Okay, okay, lass. Get ye panties out of their wad. Intelligence, huh? Tell Frank, what in the heck does that mean?"

The waitress stepped up at that moment, putting two plates of food down on the table. She refilled their glasses. Claire took a bite of her eggs, then nodded. "You're right, this is good."

Frank pointed with his fork at his own plate. "You should have gotten the French toast." He then pointed the fork at her. "Now, what's this intelligence stuff about?"

Claire stared at the plate, her eyes narrow. "Well, from what I understand, the intelligence group will track down Mythers and the Cult. We'll figure out where the bad guys are. Ops, like Jack, will be the ones who go in there and take them out. Powers and Abilities, if it works like they want it to, is going to supply Ops with the powers necessary to defeat the bad guys." She looked up, her fork still touching her plate. "Like I said, though, they don't tell us much anymore. We're learning, and that's about it. To be honest, it's pretty boring."

Frank wasn't looking at Claire, but rather was digging into his food. When he spoke, it was through a mouthful of bread and syrup. "And what about Hades? It's been a while since I've heard anything about him, but he didn't die, I'm sure about that. What's the plan there?"

Claire shrugged and stabbed a forkful of eggs. "They don't tell me anything, Frank. I don't know if they're hunting him or not."

Frank looked up with a raised eyebrow. "If they aren't hunting him, they are making a huge mistake. Hades isn't done, and I don't think he crossed back over to our side of the Veil. Those five aren't done either. You don't get powers like that and simply give up. I hope those Alphabet Boys know what they're doing."

Claire sighed. "I hope so too, but all I do is go to class now. I don't even get to see Marissa or Jack that much. How's Al doing? Have you seen him lately?"

Frank raised a finger in the air. "That's point number one that those jokers are still alive. If that witch had died, most likely Al wouldn't be annoying me so freakin' much all the time. He would tell ye that he's doing well, though I beg to differ."

"Where is he?" Claire asked.

"He went out to the west coast while I came up here. We're supposed to meet back home in another week."

Claire smiled. "You're going to spend that much time with me?"

Frank looked down at his plate, but Claire could see he was hiding a smile. "I'll see ye when I have the time, lass, but I've got a lot of things to do up here. Friends and whatnot."

Claire shook her head, still grinning. "Nope. You came here for me, and we're going to get some good hangout time in, whether you like it or not."

Frank gave a fake groan. "Zeus, save me."

Claire lay in her bed that night, different feelings running through her. She had really enjoyed her time with Frank today. She missed him when he was gone, though she respected his desire to not spend too much time at a university that was actively hunting his kind. The university was respecting it now too, not asking Claire to do anything she didn't feel comfortable with.

However, that wasn't the only thing she felt. She was bored. She'd grown accustomed—or maybe even addicted —to the fights and near-death experiences. Now her days were filled with nothing but learning, and not of the fun kind that she thought Jack and Marissa were getting. Jack was using his hands to pummel people, Marissa learning how to shoot flames from hers.

Claire knew she couldn't complain too much since this was better than the alternative of what awaited if she quit and went home. Plus, it seemed like they'd learned their lesson about trying to force her to do things she didn't want. Yet...

She was bored and didn't know what to do about it.

The knock on her door was light, as if whoever was on the other side didn't want anyone besides her to hear it.

It's certainly not Frank. He would have just teleported in.

Claire didn't feel any fear. Those days were behind her; no one was trying to hunt her down and kill her anymore. So she swung her legs off the bed and grabbed a robe from her tiny closet. She wrapped it around herself and then peered through the peephole.

Her lips curled into a smile, and she wasted no time in opening the door. "What are you two doing here?"

Jack and Marissa stood on the other side of the door.

"Let us in," he said, "before we get caught. I'm way too popular now to be hanging out with the likes of you two. I've got a reputation to uphold."

Claire shook her head, unable to pull her grin off her face. It'd been over a month since the three of them had been able to sit down with each other.

Jack let Marissa go in first, quipping, "Age before beauty" once she was in the room. Claire flipped on the light and shut the door behind them.

"Nice digs," Jack commented as he looked at the larger room.

Marissa simply gave Claire a hug. "I've missed you."

Claire hugged her back. "Not as much as I've missed you, I'm sure."

They released each other, and Claire looked at Jack. "You want one too. I know ya do."

Jack waved the hug away, sitting down in the chair next to the window as he'd done when they first met. He propped his legs up on her desk. "No hug necessary."

Claire walked over to the desk and slapped his feet off. "You're a barbarian."

"That's the spirit." Jack grinned. "How's the intelligence

track treating you?"

Claire groaned as she sat down on the bed. "Don't make me talk about it. I'm so bored I'm thinking about ripping the Veil open just to give me something to do." She patted the bed for Marissa to sit down next to her. "I heard about the muscles, and it appears for once your legend is not overblown."

Jack raised both arms and flexed his biceps. "Yes, I'm thinking about competing in the Mr. Olympia contest."

He really was a lot bigger, his arms and shoulders having filled out. He'd been athletic before, but now he looked strong as well.

Marissa lightly slapped Claire's leg. "Don't feed his ego. What's wrong with you?"

Claire chuckled. "Yes, I'd forgotten about how hungry it is. And you? You gaining any new powers we should be worried about?"

Marissa put her hands on her lap. "I'm a lot farther along than the last time we saw each other. You can accomplish great things when it's your full-time job. They're splitting me between that and working with Dr. Mitchen on how the five might have gotten their powers."

Claire leaned back on her arms. "Can you share what you've learned?"

"We're not supposed to, but truthfully, we haven't learned anything about them yet. We honestly don't know how they got those powers." She shrugged. "Which is discouraging for the track, because if we can't figure it out, we won't be able to replicate it."

"Enough business." Claire turned her attention to Jack. "How's Sam doing?"

"Who?" Jack asked, playing dumb.

"Oh, I'll be sure to mention that you forgot who she was when I see her next," Claire responded.

Jack sat up in his chair. "No need for that now. I'm just kidding. She's good. She's in Ops too, so it allows us to hang out a good bit."

Claire looked down at his muscled forearm. "She the one who put that nasty bruise there?"

Jack waved the question away, meaning it *was* Sam who did it. "Never mind. As much as we all love each other, we didn't come here just to catch up, Claire."

She raised an eyebrow. "No?"

Jack glanced at Marissa. "Well, Sissy here is worried, but that's par for the course. I walked her over here because I'm such a gentleman."

Claire sighed and looked at Marissa. "I don't know why we continue to put up with him."

Marissa shrugged. "Because he'd die for both of us."

"Ha!" Jack laughed with no conviction whatsoever. They all knew it was true.

Marissa ignored him and kept speaking. "He's not lying, though. I came to him first because his wing is closer to mine, and I honestly don't want Dean Pritcham or anyone else to see us talking. That's why we came at night."

Claire stood up and turned so she faced the room. "What are you two talking about? This is the most boring my life has been since coming here. You're worried about what?"

Jack's eyes widened. He looked at Marissa. "Did Claire start taking stupid pills, or am I not hearing her correctly?"

"Watch it, meathead," Claire shot back. "You might be

stronger now, but I'm sure I can still whip you if I have to."

Marissa, always the mature one, ignored them both. "I don't know if they're right or wrong in changing our curriculum and pulling us away from the fieldwork we were doing. It's certainly safer for everyone, but it doesn't change the things we learned while we were out there."

Claire put her hands on her hips. "What are you getting at?"

Marissa shook her head in disbelief. "Don't you remember everything that happened, Claire? To Hades, to the witches, to the Five... You're important to their side. You're supposed to do something that is going to change the tide of this war. Our betters might have taken us out of the field, but that doesn't mean the field isn't looking for us. Or more specifically, for you."

Claire opened her mouth to say something, but no words came.

Jack spoke up. "You haven't been considering that? And they put *you* in Intelligence?"

Claire turned to look at him, wanting to say something smart but unable to come up with anything.

"We didn't come here to scare you," Marissa whispered. "I just don't think anyone's really been thinking about it. The FBI freaked out that we were captured and almost killed, so they pulled us off field duty. What if they're not considering what the other side is doing?"

Jack nodded in agreement. "Whether or not it's true, Hades thinks you're the key to all this. I have the scars to prove it."

Claire shook her head. She remembered what the witches had said, as well as what Hades had told Marissa and Jack, but she'd never thought any of it was true. She'd been out there to accomplish a mission, and nothing else had mattered. It was all nonsense thrown in her way to try to stop her. She shook her head again. "None of that was true. Those creatures, they lie. They'd do anything to get our minds off the mission."

Jack looked down at his feet and nodded. "Stupid pills. That must be what they're putting in her food." He looked up at Marissa. "Are you going to smack some sense into her or should I?"

Now Marissa patted the bed. "Sit down for a second. It's not that big a deal."

Claire did as she was told, although she felt it was a very big deal. "None of that is true," she repeated, whether to herself or the other two, she didn't know.

"Think about it, Claire," Marissa whispered. "How many times have you saved the people you care about? How many times have you beat back Mythers?"

"With your help," Claire responded. "With Jack's help and Frank's help."

Jack leaned forward, placing his elbows on his knees. "As much as I wish that were true, it ain't. Did we help? Sure. Did we make the difference in any of our battles?" He shook his head with pursed lips. "Nope. You did."

"So what?" Claire asked as she stared at him. "I'm a good leader. Fine. That doesn't mean I'm something special in this war."

Jack sighed and leaned back in his chair. "She didn't used to be this dumb, Sissy, I swear it. Or maybe I've just gotten that much smarter."

"Fat chance," Claire shot back. She gazed at Marissa.

"What are you getting at?"

Marissa looked at her lap for a second, clearly deciding how to phrase what came next. "I...I don't agree with what they did to us last year. It was too much too early, and we could have died. They realize that too now, which is why so many things have changed. However, I'm not sure this new path is the right one either." She turned her head toward Claire, her hands worrying each other. "Because this new path ignores your importance. You're different from Jack and me, and regardless of what you want to believe, *we* know there is a difference."

Jack spoke up, his boisterous nature shoved aside for a moment. "We're worried that this change in curriculum, these new tracks, might be letting Hades and whoever else is coming to grow more powerful. You remember when we beat Hades, how Remington and Lance said they thought *more* gods were coming. Zeus? We haven't heard anything else about that."

Claire leaned back on her bed, letting her legs hang off while she stared at the ceiling. "That doesn't mean they aren't working on it. Remington and Lance are beasts. They're doing their job while we're doing ours. I mean, what are you suggesting? That we go to Dean Pritcham and tell her we want back into the field because I'm some kind of destined savior? No offense, but I doubt that'll go over too well."

Jack stood up. "Hey, Claire, you sound like a wimp right now, to be honest. We killed Dracula and nearly took down a Greek god, so I don't think talking to Pritcham is going to be that big a deal. Do you disagree with what we're saying?"

Claire took in a deep breath and then slowly let it out. "I talk a lot of shit to you, Jack, but I'm not an arrogant person. What you're asking me to consider is that I might be some kind of superhero, someone meant to stop an invasion. I'm from a small town with two red lights. I can't fathom being what you're claiming I am."

Jack shrugged. "So what? Are you going to dismiss what we're saying? None of us thought we would be here, but we're here all the same."

Claire closed her eyes. "I'm not dismissing it, Jack. It's just a lot to take in at once. You could be wrong, you know? And if you are, then us trying to tell them all this would disrupt the entire war. It's not something I'm going to stand up for immediately and run downstairs to Pritcham. I need to think about it some."

Jack nodded and shoved his hands into his pockets. "Okay, then." He was quiet for a second as if deciding whether to leave or say something else. He dropped his eyes to the floor. "This isn't about us. We miss each other, but that's not why Marissa and I came. We really believe you have some major part to play in this, and we believe pulling you away from it like this is going to end up hurting people. That's all."

Jack was quiet as he walked out of the room, heading back to his dorm on the other side of the mansion. Marissa stood up from the bed. "We've got time, Claire, but Jack's right. Hades and his ilk aren't quiet right now because they're chastened. They're growing more powerful. You're going to be the one who wins or loses this, whether you want it or not."

CHAPTER TWO

Hades looked at his five minions, wondering how long his brother had been planning this. He had found out through sheer luck, and now these five in front of him...

Who were they really loyal to?

The fat man, the well-dressed man, the shape-shifting sisters, and the man who couldn't stop cursing. All of them were powerful for humans, and they had originally wanted to serve Zeus.

Hades and his group had survived the church's crumbling.

Well, not at first. The one wearing the sharp suits and speaking to an imaginary friend had died, but Hades managed to fix that. He'd brought the poor bastard back to life, not out of any positive feelings toward the man, but because he wanted this group to see his true power. He wanted them to fear him more than they loved Zeus.

It had weakened him, putting out that much energy, although he regained his strength fairly fast. Now the group had left the east coast, putting distance between himself and the wretched girl who had foiled his plans.

Getting suitable living arrangements wasn't a problem, given the network that these five had set up. For all their peculiarities and outright oddness, they were committed to this endeavor. To bringing the creatures from Hades' side of the Veil to this one. Over the last few months, he had been impressed by them.

Now in California, their house overlooked the beach Hades liked. It reminded him of Poseidon, and the sky above Zeus' territory, and Hades needed not to forget about either of them for a single moment. Someone would rule Earth, and since he was already here, why shouldn't it be him?

He'd called the five to him a few moments ago. His witch sat in the corner of the room; she was silent as usual, which was how Hades wanted her. Cerberus was lounging lazily on the floor, two of his heads staring at the newcomers while his third dozed.

Fred spoke after the group had been waiting in silence for a few minutes. "Umm, sir, did you need us for something?"

A small smirk rose on Hades' face. "Did you think I called you here just to gaze on your wondrous belly, Fred?"

Fred laughed, and Hades liked it. The man was always in good spirits, although he almost certainly would die before this was all over. All of them would because Hades had plans to put those loyal only to him in charge. But that would have to wait.

"No, sir," Fred answered. "I imagine my belly isn't the reason we're here."

Bill chimed in out of nowhere. "Fucking fatty."

"Something might be wrong with that one," Hades mused. He waved the comment away. "I called you here because I'd like to hear once more what happened when you met Zeus. Continue the story."

Andrew spoke up. "Have you heard from him?"

Hades raised an eyebrow. "Have you?"

"Nuh-nuh-no, sir," Andrew replied quickly, his eyes darting to the floor. The rest of the group eyed him, as if they couldn't believe he would ask such a question after having been brought back from the dead.

"Am I *going* to hear from him?" Hades asked.

"We..." Andrew's voice trailed off.

Coward, Hades thought.

"What the mumbling moron means," Bill interjected, "is that we're supposed to be working toward bringing Zeus over here. Right now, we're twiddling our damned thumbs, so we're wondering if Zeus is going to be pissed when he arrives."

Hades looked at the short man. *Brave, but not that smart.*

"Don't worry about Zeus right now. He'll be here soon enough, I'm sure. Tell me once more what happened when you met my brother."

Storytime, Hades thought.

CHAPTER THREE
SEVEN YEARS PREVIOUS

Hermes led the group through the mansion, and it was easy to forget they were floating in the clouds until they looked out the windows. Then the reality of the situation quickly crashed in on the five humans.

Hermes was quiet as they walked, looking decidedly ridiculous in his spandex and dunce cap. The only one of the five who didn't seem particularly worried was Bill. His eyes appeared huge behind his thick glasses, and he was looking the place over as if he might want to burn it down.

Jess stepped up next to him. "Bill? You okay?"

Bill didn't turn toward her as he followed Hermes. "What do you know about him?"

"The little guy?" Jess asked.

Bill nodded.

Jess shrugged. "He's an emissary for the gods who can move between worlds easily. That's about it. And that Zeus got pissed and shrank him recently. Why?"

Bill stopped walking, letting the rest of the group go forward and forcing Jess to slow down with him. "Even *he* is more powerful than us. Look, none of us know where we are right now, but we do know we're not on Earth anymore. At least back home, I could buy a gun or something if I was overmatched. Here? I can't do anything to these creatures. They're gods, even that shrunken little bitch up there." He nodded toward the group's leader. "Everyone is super happy we've been pulled over, but we know almost fucking nothing about this place. Those dumbasses up there need a bit more fear put into them if you ask me."

Jess gazed at Bill for a moment, the look on her face saying he was quite possibly insane but probably right as well. After a moment, she turned and caught up with the group, while Bill stayed farther behind, still looking at every piece of furniture as if it might be a monster.

Hermes brought the group to a room that could only be considered fantastical by human standards. It appeared to be made of glass, although it could very well have been an illusion of some sort. Beneath the floor where one should have seen the mountain, one stared at the ocean. Above and to the side, blue sky filled the view, with the occasional cloud floating lazily.

The five stopped walking, even Bill looking mesmerized instead of murderous.

Hermes paid the room no more attention than he had the hallways. He turned to the group. "He'll be with you shortly."

Andrew didn't look at Hermes as he spoke, unable to pull away from the magnificence of the room. "She wants to know who *he* is?"

Hermes' face grew quizzical. "Who is *she*?"

Octavia smiled at the god. "Don't worry about it. We certainly don't."

Hermes studied Andrew for another second before shaking his head. "Humans are a strange species. *He* is Zeus, of course. I know you can't possibly think I had led you to Poseidon up here in these clouds?"

Andrew walked past the god as he spoke, moving deeper into the room and studying the water beneath him. "Thanks. She was just wondering."

Hermes stared for a second longer, as if Andrew was some kind of bizarre insect. He shrugged. "He'll be in here shortly. Make yourselves comfortable." With that, the shrunken god in spandex walked from the room.

The group spread out, mostly in silence. No one sat down on the couches or bothered with what appeared to be a wet bar; rather, each one found themselves at the edge of the room, staring out at the sky.

Eventually, a deep voice filled the room, causing everyone to turn to the doorway. "Do you like the views?"

No one said anything. They simply stared. It was hard to believe, despite everything they'd done up to this point, that they were staring at a Greek god. It looked as if he'd just walked off a movie screen or stepped from an old comic book. He was draped in a toga, and his right shoulder looked more like a boulder than flesh and blood. His hair was white and long, his beard the same. His eyes were an intense blue, and his forearms were adorned with golden armor.

He stepped farther into the room. "Poseidon sometimes argues that his underwater lair is more beautiful, but that's nonsense. Once you get down to the depths he lives at, it's all black anyway. Might as well go visit Hades." He moved across the room to a couch, reclining on it and throwing his legs up. His feet were bare. "Please, have a seat."

The five obviously didn't know what to do, but Fred moved forward first and sat on a chair across from the god. The other four followed his lead and sat down, although no one said anything. It was as if individually and collectively, they had reached their ability to process any more information.

Zeus eyed the five of them as if they were delicious fruit he wanted to devour. "You don't know how long I've been waiting for people like you. Or you, actually. You thought you were looking for me, or this—" he stretched his hands out to indicate the world, "but I've been looking for you all much, much longer. In fact, had I not been looking for you, I doubt you would have searched for me."

Fred's hands rested on his ample stomach. "I hate to interrupt, sir. Do we call you 'sir?'"

Zeus waved away the question. "You can call me what you wish."

Fred nodded and smiled sheepishly. "Well, I hate to interrupt, but what do you mean?"

Zeus' smile was broad, his teeth like perfectly formed white rocks. "I've been trying to reach your kind for thousands of years, Fred—"

"You know my name?" the fat man interrupted.

Bill spoke up. "He just floated your fat ass here on a cloud. I think if he can manage that, he can probably manage your name."

Zeus chuckled and his voice rumbled across the room, sounding eerily similar to thunder. "You five are going to be great. No doubt about it. Feisty creatures, you humans are. But yes, Fred, I've been trying to reach your species. What do you think the cave drawings were? It was me trying to contact your kind, but you didn't have the ability to understand yet."

The five people in the room looked confused. The wider world on Earth had not heard of a Veil, Mythers, or any of the things that would come later, but these five were farther along than the rest. They didn't understand everything, not at this point, but they had understood enough to get *here*. Every single one of them believed—as most of Earth would—that the creatures on *this* side of the Veil existed only because humans had imagined them at some point.

Which meant what Zeus just said was...

"Preposterous," Andrew said. " There isn't any way you contacted primitive humans because *you* didn't exist until *we* created you."

Zeus grew very serious, his shaggy white eyebrows drooping over his eyes and his smile falling away. He stared at each of them, looking as if death might shoot from his eyes in the form of lightning bolts. A long moment of tension passed, then he tilted his head back, and huge billows of laughter rumbled up from his chest.

He slapped his hand down on the couch, tears leaking from his eyes, and a thunderclap echoed across the room. He sat up, wiped them away, and slowly got himself under control. "Oh, that was good. I haven't laughed that hard in a long while. Thank you. I needed that." He sat up a little straighter, meeting their eyes again. "You did not create me. You did not create any of the creatures in my world, and my world is large. Much larger than you can imagine right now."

He stood up and walked over to the window, his back a hulking mass of muscle. "There are things here you probably can't imagine, and you would say, 'But someone did. Someone imagined it, and that's why it's here.'" He shook his head. "The truth is, I'm not sure how you know about us. Perhaps it is the same way I know about you. I *can* say I gave some of them to you—all the Greek gods are me, plus some of the Roman ones, but no one really likes hanging out with them over here."

He turned around and looked at the group. "Either way, we have existed much longer than you."

Octavia raised her hand, clearly not wanting to get another look like before. " That just doesn't seem possible. That would mean you have technology over here that doesn't exist on our planet."

Zeus shrugged, looking unconcerned. "We have technology here that I don't understand. Could there be crossover? Could some of your ideas have popped up over here? Perhaps. They don't concern me, those details, nor have they ever. Much of my world, my universe, was here before you, and I was as well. Whatever arguments you might have, I am the reason for those cave drawings. I am the reason for those who say they've been contacted by gods or aliens or whatever it was they told your kind. Do you understand that?"

Whether all five believed this man with long hair who lived in the sky was inconsequential. At that moment, their fear outweighed any need to be right. Each simply nodded in response.

Zeus clapped his hands, and the thunderous sound caused the humans to jump. "Good. I don't do details, and it bores me to prattle on about them. We've got more important things to discuss here, much more."

He walked back over to the couch and laid down once more, his attitude nonchalant again. "You people are going to break that pesky Veil for me. You and whoever else you can recruit."

Andrew unbuttoned his suit coat. "She says it is not possible to break the Veil."

Zeus raised an eyebrow but smiled at the same time. "I like you, Andrew. I like that little thing you have in your head too. A lot of your kind would call you crazy, but you keep things interesting." He lowered his eyebrow. "However, the thing in your head is wrong on this point. The Veil *can* be broken. I have the technology to do it, but the damned thing won't work on this side. Only on yours, and that is why you coming here is so important."

CHAPTER FOUR

H ades slammed his hand down on the chair. "ENOUGH!"

Jess had been speaking, but her mouth clamped shut.

Hades shook his head and stood up. Cerberus raised two heads and looked at his master. "Zeus talks too damned much. He always has, and I can't stand it. He went to war with our father when he could have just talked him to death. I honestly have no idea how you put up with it over there. I would have run at one of those windows full speed and jumped out, screaming with joy all the way down." He stopped walking and looked at them. "I think I've figured this out. I'm going to ask very direct questions, and I want very direct answers. Understood?"

All five nodded with wide eyes.

These humans are pets, Hades thought. *That's why Zeus wants to come over here. They're powerless and will do whatever you tell them.*

He raised one finger. "First, he gave you a piece of technology and sent you over here to start breaking the so-called Veil, yes?"

All five nodded.

He raised a second finger. "He pointed you to the first few people he knew would be able to see those from the other side?"

More nods.

Finally, a third finger. "The Veil has to be destroyed before he can come over?"

They all shook their heads decisively. *No.*

Hades lowered his hand. "Then why am I here and he's not? What's he waiting for?" It was obvious to the god that none of them wanted to speak. "Please don't make me burn one of you alive. It's tiresome and unnecessary at this juncture."

Bill spoke, his voice somehow not shaking. "He said there was someone who could stop him. A human. He didn't know who they were or where they were located, but he was sure someone would rise to challenge him. It was our job to create chaos. To bring over as many creatures as possible because then he could—"

Hades finished his sentence. "Identify her. My brother has a lot of faults, but idiocy isn't one of them. He's a wily bastard. He knew that once things started going wrong, the humans would organize, and this person would rise to the top." He paused, looking up from the floor. "But you five were looking for someone specific, were you not? Wasn't it my brother?"

Octavia shook her head. "He said he'd come when he was ready. Our job was to create chaos and to search for one creature specifically."

Hades turned to face her. "Out with it. Who?"

"Ares."

Hades' hands turned to fists and fire blazed in his eyes. *Of course. Of course he would call Ares over here.* "Either Ares would kill this special human, or he would die in the process but weaken her enough so that when Zeus arrived, he could kill her. That sum it up?" His voice was low with rage.

More nods, but not a word was spoken.

"How close were you to finding my nephew Ares?"

Fred stretched his hands above his head, forcing a fake yawn as he spoke. "Well, we have him—ahhhh." He lowered his hands and glanced to his sides as if he'd said nothing.

Hades brought his hand up to his forehead and shielded his eyes. His hand was shaking. "Ares, God of War, is here?"

Fred's eyes opened wide as if he didn't know what Hades was talking about. Jess elbowed him sharply, then filled the silence. "That's the thing. He didn't want to come, and he's much stronger than anyone else we've attempted pulling over. We're talking days of Zeus' machine pulling him. We almost had him over here, but then you showed up, so we turned the machine off. He's kind of in limbo right now."

Hades didn't remove his hand from his head. "Can you explain this term 'limbo' for me, please?" His words were polite, but his voice was filled with violence.

Bill stood up and stomped to the other side of the room, speaking as he went. "No damn games in this place, and now I have to explain fucking words. 'Limbo' means the Veil isn't what Zeus thought. It's not what Earth thinks either, at least not fully. There is a barrier, but you can get stuck in it. There's a lot of creatures stuck in it right now, I imagine, and when it finally falls, they'll rain down on us. Either way, your nephew is stuck because you showed up." He stopped walking, his back to the crew.

Hades slowly let his hand fall. The short man still didn't turn around, and Hades knew why. He was scared to death. Hades decided to ignore the little outburst for now. Couldn't go around killing someone every time they got mad. That was Ares' habit.

Hades retreated to his chair and sat down. He stared at the floor, ignoring Cerberus as he came over to lick his hand. He heard the short man patter back over to the couch but paid him no mind. After a moment, he asked, "How much does Zeus know about what is happening over here?"

"We don't know," someone answered. Hades didn't care who.

Ares was stuck, and Zeus was probably in the dark about a lot of this. Hell, Hades hadn't even known Earth existed until all his workers disappeared. Zeus also knew about this girl, the one with a hat much like Hades', and he was scared of her. The Veil had broken enough now that Hades had been able to step through, yet Ares was stuck in it. Or maybe he was simply stuck because the bastard was stubborn and didn't want to come. Either way, this firmed up Hades' plans.

Zeus wasn't getting dominion over this place. Hades was. Yet, his brother wasn't an idiot, and unleashing Ares on that girl was still the best move. Hades would let Ares handle his dirty work, and after she was dispatched, Hades would ensure that the moment Zeus crossed over... Well,

Hades had never shed a tear about what happened to their father. So what if the same thing happened to his brother?

He smiled, and the flames in his eyes flickered. He looked at his five minions. They were terrified of him, and rightly so. They didn't know Ares, though, or what he would unleash on this world. Hades smiled wider. "Let's go ahead and bring my nephew over. It's been far too long since I've seen him."

It took a week to have the artifact brought to them, but the minions had an exceptional network of people dedicated to their cause. Now it sat in front of Hades, a black orb about the size of a human head. It was round and appeared to have no imperfections, but it didn't look like something Zeus would create. The God of Lightning preferred sky blue, not night black.

"How many of these instruments did he give you?" Hades asked.

Octavia walked to the black orb but didn't touch it. "He gave us one. This one."

Hades shook his head. "You already told me the FBI has one of these things, that another of your group was using."

Octavia smiled but didn't look at the god. "We pulled one through the Veil when we got back. We wanted to see if it was possible and if what Zeus had said was true. We hadn't imagined anything like this, but he handed it to us. Sure enough, we were able to find one."

Hades mentally dismissed the conversation. He didn't really care how many black orbs were floating around the world or whether they could bring more over. Right now, his nephew was what mattered. "You start this instrument, and then you'll be able to bring him over?"

Octavia nodded without smiling. The rest of the group stood against the wall. Hades wasn't sure if they were geniuses or fools, but he thought probably the latter because they had been about to bring over Ares by themselves. He would have as soon slit their throats as soon as he said hello. "One of you needs to stay here with me and operate it. The others should scatter like the wind, as long as you remain on the premises."

"Why?" Bill asked.

Hades didn't bother to glance at him. "Because Zeus said he hated Ares worse than all the other gods due to his arrogance and brutality. It's best that my nephew not see you as soon as he arrives."

Fred pushed off the wall with a smile. "No *problemo*. Octavia, you got this, right?"

The woman was still in her black-skinned form, although Hades understood she was a shapeshifter. "Leave, big boy. I'll bring him over."

"Good enough for me," Fred responded before heading to the door.

Hades didn't look as the rest of them left the room. He waited until the door was closed before speaking again. "Once you get done bringing him over, I'm going to suggest you go where they went and leave my nephew and me to speak."

Octavia nodded and stepped back from the orb. Hades watched her carefully, unsure of what was happening. The orb began to emit bolts of lightning, and for a moment,

Hades wondered if he might have been tricked. If perhaps she was pulling Zeus over. He stepped forward, ready to kill her, but paused when a wall of electricity shot across the room.

He turned his head to the right and watched as a leg appeared through it, then a torso, and finally a Greek god. The orb quit working and the lightning died. "You should leave now," he whispered to the woman.

Her footsteps fled across the room, then the door swung shut behind her.

The god in front of Hades stood over six feet tall and had an athletic frame. He wore battle-ready armor and held a sword in his right hand. His eyes were full of rage, focused on the door Octavia had just left through. He stepped forward, obviously knowing who was in front of him but not caring at that moment. Hades knew his kin, but the younger god didn't know where he was or how he'd gotten here. All he cared about was killing the person he thought responsible for bringing him.

Yes, Hades thought. *Zeus was clever. Bring him over and kill the one who rises, then hop over and own the world before any of his brethren knew about it.*

"Welcome, nephew." Hades grinned. "Do not worry about her too much just yet. Trust me, there are more formidable foes to conquer."

CHAPTER FIVE

Remington stared at the screen with a growing sense of fear. He had felt that other times during this wild endeavor of the Veil tearing, but not when looking at a *screen*. "That isn't possible."

The meeting was classified as top secret. He sat next to Lance, both of them staring at a large flat-screen television that was connected to a secure computer. A person sat behind the computer; Remington had been told his name but no longer remembered it. The person heading up this meeting was none other than the FBI Director, Charles Manning. Neither Remington nor Lance had met the man before this, despite their position in the Veil operation.

To be sitting in front of him now added another layer of fear over what the screen was showing.

The director used a laser pointer, shining a green dot over the red ones that covered the television. A map of the world was displayed on it, the red dots showing up both on land and in the water. "Things have changed rapidly over the past six weeks. The CIA monitors incidents of Veil crossings worldwide, as you both know, although we only deal with the domestic incidents. It can be a bitch coordinating between different agencies, and that's why you're just now seeing this. There's a global team working on it, but that's not why I've called you here today."

He turned his body so that one shoulder faced the agents and the other the screen. "The Veil is tearing at an unprecedented rate, and worse, it's happening faster. As you can see, it's not just over land. We've got giant squid falling into the Pacific Ocean and great white whales into the Indian Ocean, and I don't even know what to call what we saw appear off the coast of Japan." He was quiet for a second, and without looking over, said, "There are rumors about a large reptilian creature coming out of the ocean."

He nodded to the man behind the computer, and the screen switched to a map of the US. The dots were tenfold what Remington or Lance knew to be the case. "The media is reporting on it, but there aren't any official numbers except for this, gentleman." He turned to look at the two agents. "Speaking frankly, I and the best minds in the world believe the Veil will soon have torn completely. I could list every monster and fairytale creature that's come across, but I'll leave that for your research."

Remington raised his hand. "Question, sir."

The director looked at the screen. "Go ahead."

Remington continued, "While some of our job is intelligence, the vast majority has been recruitment and operations. Do we not have agents better suited to deal with this information?"

The director turned his laser pointer off and faced the two agents. "Recruitment is done, gentlemen. That's what the map behind me is saying. We were preparing for the long term, but there might not be a long term for humanity if this isn't stopped. I asked you here today because the screen behind me isn't the only information we've gathered. You were both part of the early operation that captured one of the instruments we thought was being used to bring Mythers through the Veil. That is true. That black orb *can* pull creatures across, but it can also send creatures from our side to the other."

Remington was stunned. He turned to Lance, but his partner couldn't even return the glance. He was staring at the director with a furrowed brow. Lance spoke. "Sir, we weren't aware of any progress. I want to make sure I understand what you're saying. We can both pull creatures over and send them back?"

The director nodded, folding his hands. "Theoretically, but that's not what I'm considering. We have one orb, and while we *think* we can operate it, we've had limited success in the laboratory. There isn't any way we'll be able to use this thing to send Mythers back through the Veil in any mass operation."

Remington felt lost. "Sir, I'm not following what you're asking us to do."

The director met his eyes, seriousness taking over the room. "We'd like to send someone across and then attempt to bring them back."

"Why?" Lance asked.

"We need to know if there's anything we can learn over there. We think this invasion is going to be complete within a month. If there is anything we can gain from crossing over, we need it immediately."

Remington put his hands on the table. "Are you asking Agent Lance and me to go?"

The director shook his head. "We're not going to put anyone on the team in unnecessary danger. The FBI would like the two of you to convince the leprechaun to go. Frank."

Remington's eyes narrowed. "You're sure you can bring him back?"

"No," the director responded. "We're not sure of much right now. I'm meeting with the head of Justice and the President this afternoon. The leprechaun Myther seems to feel some loyalty to the human species, and he might be able to find out information that can help us. If we can't bring him back, then we just sent him home. No harm, no foul."

Remington let out a sigh. "With all due respect, Director Manning, you don't know Frank."

Frank watched the two agents enter the bowling alley and thought, *Do they own any other clothes?* They wore the same suits they'd worn the day he'd first seen them a year ago. He sighed and grabbed the pitcher of beer in front of him, filling his glass nearly to the rim. It was swill, but he didn't care at this point. He knew whatever these two were about to say would not be good, at least not for him.

The FBI agents reached the table and sat down opposite Frank. The leprechaun sipped his beer without speaking.

"Thanks for agreeing to meet with us," Remington began.

Frank eyed him suspiciously over the rim of his glass. He finished his sip, set the glass down, and belched. "It's not like ye'd take no for an answer. Let's consider the formalities over with. What's this about?"

Lance leaned back in his seat. "You're not going to like it, and we want to be upfront about that."

Frank rolled his eyes. "Ye think I've liked anything you've brought me? That's a given. Spit it out."

The conversation lasted about five minutes. Frank said nothing, just sipped his beer and listened as the agents explained what they wanted. When they finished, he stared at them blankly for a few seconds. "Ye have asked me for a lot of crazy things over the past year, but this tops it all. Ye want to use one of those machines to try to send me back across the Veil, and then hope and pray ye can bring me back over here?"

Remington folded his hands on the table. "That's right. Hades is underground, but something is happening, and it's happening fast. We're hoping you can give us information we didn't have before."

Frank looked at the lane to his left. The pins were ready to be knocked down, but he didn't think he'd be bowling much more today. "What kind of information? Do ye even know?"

Remington followed his gaze to the pins. "We've given this a lot of thought, Frank, and it isn't something we really want to ask. We do know we were wrong about Mythers. It is obvious that not all of you wish us harm. Some of you—you included—are either neutral or want to help. We'd like you to go back home and find others like you who are willing to help or at least give us more information about what is happening."

Frank's brow furrowed. "Why do you think any of them will have more information? We were just as clueless about how we ended up over here as anyone else."

"We're running out of options and quickly," Lance said. "We're using every resource we currently have. Maybe no one knows, but we doubt it. This is being coordinated from somewhere. Maybe the rank and file have no clue, but there are gods over there, right? Powerful creatures? Perhaps one of them will tell you something."

"Aye." Frank took a sip of his beer and swallowed. "Or maybe they'll kill me for asking. There's that possibility. Or maybe ye can't work that little orb of yours, and I end disappearing into the ether. Lots of maybes, not a lot of surety."

Remington nodded solemnly. "You're right. We're asking you the same way we asked Claire. Humanity needs your help right now, but we can't force you to give it."

Frank flicked his glass, and it gave a soft echo. He stared at the amber liquid. "Humanity. I curse the day I found out ye existed. Does Claire know about this?"

Lance shook his head. "No. This is top secret, strictly on a need to know basis. She cannot know about it. No one at the university can. For the most part, the university is a non-entity now. The plans that we'd made for the students centered around a long-term strategy. This is no longer long-term."

Frank sighed and sank back into his chair. "Can ye tell me what the plan is if I don't go? Is there anyone else you have in mind?"

Remington shrugged, his brown eyes meeting Frank's. "Maybe Griff, if we can find him. Or the centaur you know. There are options, just none we trust as much as you."

The leprechaun waved away the compliment. "That wannabe bird is probably drunk somewhere, and the centaur doesn't know his asshole from his hoof. Send him back, and he'll probably just gallop across the plains. None of them will be able to do a damned thing for ye."

Remington put his hands in the air. "What's your answer, Frank?"

He pursed his lips. "Can I say goodbye to Claire in case ye morons mess it all up?"

Lance shook his head. "No, but you can write a letter to her and give it to us. I promise if something goes wrong, we'll make sure she gets it."

Frank looked at the ceiling, still sunk down in his chair. "The problem with ye humans isn't so much that ye don't have green skin. It's that ye prey on the good nature of us Mythers. Help us, save us, think of the children. What's a leprechaun supposed to do if he wants to remain a good person?"

Remington grinned. "Help us. Save the world. Be a hero. All that stuff."

Frank sat up and refilled his beer. He said nothing as he chugged the whole thing, and when he was finished, his belch lasted multiple seconds. He stood up and looked at the agents, his head at the same level as theirs. "I'll do it, but from now until ye send me over, I better have an IV of beer dripping into my veins. Get me a case right now, because I imagine ye two are going to make me travel."

The room consisted of white walls, white floors, and a white ceiling. There was a one-way mirror on the far wall, and Frank knew humans were watching him from the other side. In the middle of the room was a pedestal, and on it sat that Zeus-forsaken black orb.

About the size of a bowling ball, Frank thought. *Life can certainly be ironic. The thing ye love is going to kill ye.*

Remington and Lance stood on either side of the only door to the room, both of them looking as solemn as undertakers. It'd taken the group a day to get up here, and Frank had been true to his word. He had either been drinking or sleeping every second of that time.

He had a can of beer in his right hand. He raised it to the FBI agents. "Ye geniuses have any idea if this is going to make the trip with me?"

Remington gave a small chuckle. "Will it make you feel better if I say yes?"

Frank nodded. "Lie to me if ye must."

"Then sure, it'll be there when you cross over."

Frank shook his head, hardly able to believe he'd agreed to this. Hardly able to believe he'd gotten into any of this to begin with. *Too good-hearted ye are,* he thought. "Any idea where I'm going to end up?"

Remington grinned. "We've programmed it so you'll end up in a bowling alley with more beer than you know what to do with."

Frank smiled in return. "Keep the lies coming, ye bastard." He took a sip of his beer. "Okay, enough chatter. Tell the humans behind that wall to get this thing started."

Remington raised his hand and pointed at the window, giving them the go-ahead. "Remember, Frank, you've got forty-eight hours to get whatever information you can. The brains behind the wall feel they know how to bring you back, so at the end of forty-eight hours, you're out of time."

Frank belched. "The brains behind that wall are less intelligent than the ones in here if they think a leprechaun who likes to bowl is going to be able to hobnob with the elites on my side, but whatever. Let's do it."

Lance opened the door and looked back. "See you in two days, Frank."

CHAPTER SIX

F rank opened his eyes slowly, fully expecting to see
nothing but darkness.

It wasn't darkness, but it was not that much better. A
man lay sleeping on the ground, his beard and hair
stretching out dozens of feet around him. The man didn't
move from his slumber, but he gave a slight snore. He was
on his back, and his stomach was rising and sinking in a
paced rhythm.

Frank glanced at his right hand. He was holding his
beer. "Praise Zeus, at least something went right." He'd
never met the fool in front of him—who had?—but he
knew the name: Rip Van Winkle. He took a small sip of his
beer, realizing he'd have to conserve it until he could find
more.

He took in his surroundings, which were the problem.
Ole Rip had fallen asleep on a mountain, and sure enough,
that was where Frank was—on a freakin' mountain.

He shook his head and started walking. He only had
two days to get answers, and the sleeping idiot here

wouldn't have any for him. "I should have told them to send the damned centaur."

Even with teleportation, it took Frank a good bit of time to get off the mountain. He didn't have a watch; all he knew was his beer was gone long before he reached the bottom. When he got there, he was even less happy than he'd been at the top.

Dwarves, he thought as he looked around. *Wannabe leprechauns without the brains. Those FBI agents are gonna pay if they ever get me back to Earth.*

There was nothing to look at aboveground because dwarves lived beneath it. Frank saw one of the entrances to their dwellings about thirty feet away, and he had a choice: go bang on the door or keep walking and try to find someone else. The decision was pretty easy because while dwarves were leprechaun impostors, they made a decent brew.

Frank walked over to the entrance. Within was a dirt path that descended slowly for about five feet, and at the end was an iron door that was only slightly above Frank's height. Obviously this was for protection since it would be hard for a giant to get in.

Frank raised his hand and banged hard. An echo made its way through the tunnels beyond the door until he could hear it no more. He waited. He knew the dwarves. If he waited long enough, the stubby creatures would show up.

He was right. A small slot in the iron door slid open,

and two heavily browed eyes stared at him. "What business do you have here, leprechaun?"

Frank groaned internally. Stubborn creatures and cautious. Worst place in the world he could be right now. "I need to talk to yer king immediately."

One of the eyebrows went up. "Oh, is that so? I shall go get him right away."

The slot began closing, and Frank whipped his hand up to stop it. He knew what he had to do here, and it was something he'd swore he would never, ever do. It went against his very nature, his *genetics*, yet dwarves and leprechauns were similar in one fashion: they hoarded wealth. "Ye let me see the king, and I'll give ye me pot."

The force on the slot stopped. The dwarf on the other side knew exactly what he meant. Frank had gotten his pot of gold a long, long time ago, and he was offering to hand it over to meet this dwarf king.

The eyes on the other side of the door narrowed. "There's only one way someone can get your gold, leprechaun, and we both know it. You have to be captured."

Frank didn't take his hand from the slot but sighed. "I'm well aware, ye moron. I have to be caught. I know ye don't have the brains of me big toe, but think this through. Throw some chains on my arms and bring me inside the door, and I'm caught. All I'm asking is that you honor your word and bring me to your king."

He could tell the dwarf was thinking, but he saw the greed in the creature's eyes. "How big is your pot, leprechaun?"

Frank felt his heart breaking. "You'll need a dungeon

down here to hold it all." He took his hand off the slot. He knew the dwarf wouldn't be able to help himself.

The slot closed and long minutes passed, but Frank didn't move. Eventually he heard the locks on the other side of the door moving, and then it swung open. Four dwarves dressed in battle gear and holding axes with short handles stood before him. The lead one held manacles in his left hand. "Put these on, leprechaun."

Frank eyed the manacles. "You'll honor your deal? You'll take me to your king?"

The dwarf didn't so much as smile back. "We aren't your kind. You don't have to capture us to make us honor a deal. You put these on, and you'll see our king."

Claire, you'll never know how much I care about you, Frank thought as he mentally imagined his pot of gold filling these creatures' coffers. He offered his hands and felt the cold chains of poverty slap over his wrists.

The dwarf finally smiled. "This way, leprechaun." He led Frank into the bowels of the earth.

The king was about an inch taller than everyone else and twice as wide. He had broad shoulders, a thick chest, and a stomach that matched both in its swell. He sat on a throne that was much smaller than the chairs Frank had grown accustomed to on the other side of the Veil.

He stared at Frank with confident eyes, not distrustful at all. That was because he knew he could kill the leprechaun in the blink of an eye. His guard circled the room, all battle-ready, and Frank was wearing khaki shorts and a beach shirt.

The king stroked his beard as he spoke. "You gave up a lot to see me, leprechaun, and with no guarantees other than to have a chat. When your chat is over, you fill my coffers. Is that understood?"

Frank knew that smart-ass remarks wouldn't get him anywhere right now, but he still couldn't bring himself to grovel to this wannabe leprechaun. "It's understood."

"Great," the king responded happily. "Talk. What brought you to my door in such a ridiculous looking outfit?"

Frank started his story, knowing that time was short but details were necessary if he had any hope of these creatures helping him. He talked until his mouth was dry and he would have cut his right pinky off for a beer. The room was silent as he did, listening intently, and when he finished, the king only stroked his beard for long minutes.

Frank couldn't take it anymore. "Well?"

The king smiled. "Well, that's an interesting tale. I'm inclined to believe it since the rumors of different creatures going missing have reached my ears. I even heard a rumor that the underworld was empty, and I'm considering taking it over. Would be very roomy compared to this. Let's say I do believe you. What do you want from me?"

Frank squeezed his eyes shut. This was the tough part. If they did him the favor, where would he go? If anyone had any idea what was happening here, who would it be? Who could and would help? He opened his eyes, ready to take a chance. "I know dwarves have machinery. I've heard you even have flying machines. I want you to take me to Poseidon. If anyone will know what's going on, it's him."

The king stroked his long beard, still grinning. "You'd like me to lend you use of one of our most highly coveted machines and take you across the realms to a Greek god I've never met. That's about right?"

Frank nodded. "This won't stop with Earth." He pointed at the king. "Because whoever is arranging this only wants power. They couldn't get it here, but once they have another world under their control, do you think they won't want this one as well?"

The king waved away the thought as if it were an annoying fly. "Never mind that, leprechaun. Us dwarves have fought dragons and won. Another war doesn't frighten me. Do you have any other reason I might take you there? Because your gold is already mine."

Frank looked at the ground. Perhaps it had been dumb to come here. Maybe he should have found a dragon and traded gold for a flight, but he was out of riches now. "Because if ye don't, people I care about are going to die."

The king laughed and looked at the guard standing next to the wall. "He talks as if I care about the people *he* cares about. You're wasting my time, leprechaun, which I hate. However, I'll let you make it up to me. I'd like a bit of entertainment right now. You're surrounded by twelve of the deadliest dwarves in my kingdom. I'll unchain you, and if you're the last person standing, we'll get you to Poseidon. If you don't like the deal... Well, we'll you show you back out."

Frank looked to his left and right. He'd seen dwarves battle before, but had they ever seen a leprechaun fight?

These twelve creatures wore armor and held weapons, but... He shook his head, smiling inwardly. *If they had any brains, they'd be leprechauns*, he thought. Frank looked at the king. "Ye have a deal." He raised his arms up, wanting the manacles off.

The king laughed, and Frank knew right then the royalty had never fought a leprechaun. *His loss and my gain.*

An assistant moved from behind the throne with a large metal key. He stuck it into the manacle on Frank's left arm and then his right. The chain fell to the floor and the assistant stepped back. The king didn't stand but remained sitting. "I've heard leprechauns were clever creatures, but it's clear that was only rumors. Sad, really, to die like this. I hope you die well, little green one."

Frank raised an eyebrow. Those bastards were the same damned height.

He heard the footsteps of guards moving forward, closing their circle around him. He'd have to deal with the height insult later. Right now, he needed to show these dwarves why they were wannabes.

Frank squatted and grabbed the chain by one end, then stood up, draping it down by his leg. He started twirling his wrist and the chain moved with it, whipping faster and faster until it hummed in the air and could hardly be seen. He turned slowly in a circle, taking them all in. Their eyes glinted with thoughts of glory and murder—bloodlust obviously setting in on them.

Going to be lusting for some ice for ye balls in a minute, Frank thought.

He let the circle close in on him a bit more, waiting until there was less than a foot between each shoulder. His knees dropped slightly and he leaped into the air, a flash of light replacing him as he did.

He appeared behind the line, his chain still swirling, and he smashed the first dwarf he saw in the head. The helmet dented, and the creature collapsed without so much as a grunt. The two dwarves standing next to their fallen comrade turned, but much too slowly. The twirling chain bashed each in the face, breaking their noses. They both dropped their weapons, and then Frank brought the chain down on their knees, cracking both of them. They fell to the ground screaming, blood pouring from their broken faces.

Nine left, he thought. The group turned toward him as one and rushed him.

Frank pumped on the nearest dwarf's shoulder with a single light foot. The spinning chain bashed his head and then Frank was in the air again, finding another shoulder and bashing the owner's head there too. He walked across two more dwarves like that, sending them to the ground before he saw an axe somersaulting through the air at him.

Frank barely had time to teleport, the flash of light appearing just before the axe flew through it. He hadn't teleported exactly where he wanted, landing in front of a dwarf instead of behind him. The creature brought a meaty fist across Frank's face, which sent him sliding across the floor.

Those bastards are strong, he thought as he pulled himself up. They were running at him again, and though he still held his chain, he didn't have time to set it spinning.

Frank ducked as an axe swung at his head, then twirled to his left before teleporting once more.

This time the landing was perfect. He stood on top of a dwarf's shoulders, one foot on each. He hopped off behind him, bringing the chain around the creature's neck as he did. He yanked on it, and the dwarf toppled. Frank gave him a kick in the head, then picked up the unconscious man's axe.

Four dwarves stood in front of Frank, but now they looked cautious. The bloodlust in their eyes had disappeared, replaced by wariness. They moved forward, spreading out slightly. Frank saw that the king had stood up and was no longer stroking his beard.

"Ye want to call an end to this?" Frank yelled over the dwarves. "Or should I lay them low too?"

The king said nothing, and Frank shrugged. His eyes met those of one of the men in the middle. "Sorry, buddy. Yer king is making me do it."

Frank teleported once more, landed directly in front of the far left dwarf, and cracked him in the skull with the butt of the axe. Frank didn't bother to look at what happened next. He flashed once more and appeared on the far right, cracking the dwarf's kneecap. That left only two.

"ENOUGH!" the king roared. "Enough."

Frank backpedaled quickly to create separation between him and the remaining fighters. He didn't want to give them a chance for a cheap shot. He turned to the king. "Yer admitting that I won?"

The king stared at him in disgust. "You won, you little green bastard." He looked at his fallen soldiers, some unconscious and some groaning in pain. "Get them to a medic. Now."

Assistants flooded the area and began tending the

wounded. The king looked back at Frank. "I never want to see you again. I'll give you transport, but if you come back to my doors, no amount of teleporting will save you. Understand?"

Frank shrugged and smiled, still gripping the axe. "I don't like this place anyway. Smells funny. All of you down here in the ground with no ventilation, breathing each other's farts all day. Disgusting." He paused and looked at the men being pulled off, remembering something. "Oh, before I go, can ye lend me a beer or two?"

Four dwarves manned the mechanical contraption that flew Frank toward his destination. Humans had something similar to this, although they called it a helicopter, and it was much more technically advanced. This was more or less a ten by ten basket with fans attached to the top.

Frank said nothing to the dwarves as they traveled, simply watched the land pass below him. He knew his time was running short, but not by how much. Frank had asked before entering the flying machine how far away Poseidon's kingdom was, and one had grunted back that it wasn't too far. Frank hadn't thought he'd be able to get a better answer out of them, so he let it drop.

Night came, and Frank dozed on and off in the corner, not trusting the dwarves not to throw him out of the basket. When the sun rose, one of them gave him a rough kick, waking from his slumber. "We're here, leprechaun."

Frank groggily rose to his feet. He wiped his eyes and peered over the rim. They were indeed *somewhere*. "That's water down there. What do you expect me to do, dive in?" Beneath Frank was nothing but blue ocean. Frank could see the outlines of a beach far away, but he probably couldn't get any help there.

"Not our problem," one of the dwarves responded. "You wanted to get to Poseidon. He lives down there."

Frank stared at the ocean and quickly realized how much trouble he was in. *Ye didn't think this through, moron.* What in the hell was he supposed to do? "Well, ye see, lads, I sort of thought there might be a door or convoy or something might help me make me way down to the bottom. Us leprechauns, we're not such strong swimmers, if ye'll have me be honest with ye."

The dwarves looked at each other with shock on their faces, then they laughed as one.

"The king is going to love hearing this," one of them said. He turned to Frank. "That's not our problem, leprechaun. Now, you can either jump, or we can help you jump. Choice is yours."

Frank tried to swallow, but his mouth was dry. This was the dumbest thing he'd ever done in his whole life, bar none. He glanced at the four dwarves and saw they were serious. He knew he could take them easily, but then what? He didn't know how to fly this thing, and it wouldn't run forever.

Claire, I hope me luck hasn't run out, lass, he thought. *And if it has, I hope ye can send me some of yours.*

Frank took in a deep breath, grabbed the rail, and leaped out of the flying machine.

He hit the water, and after flailing for a bit, welcomed the cold darkness as he went under.

CHAPTER SEVEN

Hades sat in the back of a heavily tinted black stretch SUV. The five had procured it for him before they began their cross-country drive. They'd actually gotten two SUVs. Hades had never spent a lot of time with his nephew for obvious reasons, but the past few days had shown him the young god wasn't what one would call stable. Stuffing him in a vehicle with too many people would end in bloodshed.

The drive had been long because Hades was taking them across the country to the humans' capital, Washington, DC.

They were about an hour out of the city when Bill finally spoke up. "What is the plan?"

It was one of the few times the man had spoken without vulgarity. Hades sort of liked the weird-looking human. He had some mental problems, but that pretty much went for everyone in his crew. Hades imagined he wasn't cursing now because he was scared out of his mind.

He sat on the far right side of the SUV's back row and

stared out the window as he spoke. "We're going to let humanity know who is in charge now."

Bill pointed to the SUV in front of them. "You're going to let that damned psychopath loose is what you're saying?"

Hades nodded with a slight grin. "That's correct."

Bill dropped his hand and remained quiet. Hades wondered what the humans had thought would happen when they tried to bring gods to this world. Did they think there would be parades and such? "You wanted a war. Wars are won with blood. Today, we strike first blood."

Andrew was wearing his business suit as always and sitting on the row in front of Hades. "She wants to know if your dog is going to fight as well?"

Cerberus was riding with Ares. As violent and deadly as the god was, Hades didn't think he'd give the pup any trouble. "I haven't decided yet."

Fred sat facing Hades' seat, taking up two spaces. "Are we going to fight?"

Hades finally smiled. "You really don't get it, do you? You saw me go up against that girl and think that humanity has a chance of winning this thing. If Zeus was right, and she is fated to stop us, then that is the only reason I didn't kill her then. But if it's only she who is meant to stop us, then the rest of you?" He shook his head, still grinning. "No, Fred. There won't be any reason for you to fight, not unless you want to."

The two SUVs rolled into a parking structure. It was a very different-looking area than what Hades had witnessed driving into the city. "What is this? Why are there so many metal chariots here and no people?"

Octavia stifled a smile. "The people are in the buildings we saw while driving here. Did you decide whether you want to visit Congress or the White House yet?"

Hades ignored Octavia's stifled smile. He pursed his lips as he thought. "Which has more people in it?"

Octavia shook her head. "That's not how you should think about this. It's the importance of the people that matters. If someone killed all your servants, would it matter as much as killing you?"

Hades' brow furrowed, and he looked at the front seat. That was one of the smartest questions this group of fools had ever asked. "No, it wouldn't matter, obviously. I'm a god, and they're ghosts. But it would be insulting, as you clearly saw when I came over to get them back. Why do you ask that question?"

Octavia turned around and looked at him. "Both places hold important people. Congress is less important, although there are more of them. The President is in the White House. He is the most important person in the United States, and maybe the world."

Hades stroked his chin with his right hand. "So if I kill this President, that will be the most shocking thing I can do?"

Octavia's eyes widened as if the thought that this might happen was finally dawning on her. "If you kill the President, the entire world is going to lose its collective mind."

Hades didn't understand all of humanity's phrases. "So, killing this President will be shocking?"

Jess gave a high laugh. "To say the *very* least, yes."

Hades nodded, satisfied. "Then that is where we shall go. Can we walk there from here, or should we park at that house?"

Now Fred laughed, his belly shaking mightily. "Parking probably isn't the best idea."

"Why not?" Hades asked.

Bill turned around now. "It's fucking *guarded*. Guarded in, like, if you look suspicious walking up to it, they'll throw you in jail."

"Plus," Octavia said with less anger, "There are no parking spots."

Hades paused for a moment, staring at the humans, who were all looking at him as if he were Medusa. They really didn't get it. They thought rules applied to him. That the god in the other vehicle might somehow lose this battle at this house painted white. "Okay, we're going to the White House. Is there a lawn?"

Everyone's eyes were wide as the five faces nodded at him. "Park on the lawn, then. Driver, do you hear me?"

"Yes, sir," came the reply. The driver said something into the two-way radio he carried, communicating with the other vehicle. The SUV reversed out of the parking spot, and the five humans slowly turned around, although the expressions on their faces didn't change.

They're terrified, Hades thought. *They won't be in a few minutes.*

The drive to the White House was short, and when they arrived, Fred pointed at it. "That's it, and that's the lawn. To get onto it, we'll need to drive through those fences. The moment you do, you're going to have people shooting at both vehicles."

Hades frowned. The house wasn't far away, hundreds of feet at most. No need to drive onto the lawn. "Let's just stop here."

No one said anything. They were too scared to speak.

"Stop the car," Hades demanded. It screeched to a halt, and Hades grabbed the door handle. "Wait here. I need to talk to Ares."

He picked up his helmet from the seat and set it on his head, then stepped out of the vehicle. He walked at a leisurely pace to the chariot behind them and pulled the back door open. Cerberus hopped up, and all three heads yelped happily to see their master. Ares glared with steel-colored eyes. "I'm tired of riding in these things. Your dog stinks, too."

Hades ignored the jab about Cerberus. Loud noises were coming from the chariots, what Fred had called a 'horn' on the way over here. Hades ignored them. "We're done riding, nephew. It's time to fight." He turned to his left and pointed at the target building. "Go there and make war. Kill anyone who tries to stop you."

Ares' eyes narrowed as he looked past his uncle. He didn't smile at what he saw, but a look of contentment replaced the anger. He glanced at Hades. "You coming?"

Hades shrugged. "I might help, but I don't think you'll need it. Go on and have fun."

Ares looked at the dog inside the car. "I think he would enjoy it too."

Hades raised an eyebrow. His nephew liked the dog, despite his angry comment earlier. "You can take him. Cerberus, go with Ares."

The dog's heads all yelped happily again. Hades stepped

back from the vehicle and Ares climbed out, stretching his frame to its full six-feet-four-inches. He carried his sword in his right hand and a shield in his left. He wore silver gauntlets on his arms and legs, plus a metal chest plate. He hadn't brought his helmet, but he wouldn't need it here.

Hades looked into the sky. "I guess you don't have your birds."

Now Ares smiled. "They're here, Uncle. They crossed over before I did, and they've been flying to get to me since I arrived." He glanced at the sky as well, turning around so he faced the vehicle. "There they are now."

And sure enough, Hades saw a large flock racing across the sky. They were still a ways off yet, but at their current speed, it wouldn't take them long to get there. "Do you want to wait for them?"

Ares shook his head as he turned back to the building. "No. They will make for a nice surprise in a few minutes."

The horns were growing louder, and people were now getting out of their cars. They were screaming at the SUVs. Perhaps some of them could see Ares, although Hades was invisible at this point. Hades stepped out of the way allowing Ares and Cerberus to march toward the gates. He eyed the metal chariots and screaming humans, who were enraged that someone would stop on their roads.

In a few minutes, they would be crying and bleeding. Hades smiled at the thought. He walked to his SUV and got into the back seat. No one looked at him as he sat down. Their eyes were trained on the god and the dog approaching the gates.

Hades found the button they had shown him earlier, and he rolled down the window. Ares had stopped in front of the gate and seemed to be studying it. Hades saw movement coming toward his nephew, men with guns drawn. If Ares saw them, he didn't pay them any attention.

The god shrugged and wedged his shield between the fence rails. He pushed, and the metal gave way as if it had the consistency of cheese.

"STOP RIGHT NOW!" one of the men shouted, his pistol raised and pointed at the god.

Ares turned to him, his face calm as if someone had only called his name. He stared for a second, unsure what was being pointed at him, and then stepped through the now-open gate. Cerberus jumped after him quickly. Men were streaking across the lawn with high-powered automatic rifles raised, and they began firing simultaneously.

The bullets *should* have hit Ares, but when they touched his body, they disintegrated into puffs of ash. He didn't speed up or even look at the ten-plus men now firing at him. Cerberus took off, and it appeared that none of the men saw him at first—not until he was ripping their throats out with one of his heads. He pounced from man to man, each one too slow to realize what was happening until it was too late.

Ares continued walking as the last guard fell dead behind him. Sirens wailed into the sunlit sky, and traffic had come to a standstill. More men rushed the lawn, one reaching Ares before Cerberus could get him. He swung a knife at the god's face—

All five humans in the SUV gasped. They'd never seen *anything* move that fast. It was as if Ares' arm didn't move but teleported. One moment the knife was about to cut him, and the next, the guard lay on the ground with his head bashed in from the shield.

Ares didn't even pause.

"Is he going to walk right into the White House?" Octavia whispered.

Hades chuckled. "What did you expect him to do? Wait outside for someone to give him an invitation?"

No one said anything. They simply watched the carnage taking place on the other side of the fence.

Police on foot and the flock of birds arrived at the same time. Hades pointed at the birds as they streaked down from the sky. "Watch."

Their feathers shot from their bodies as if slung by bows, but they moved with *purpose.*

It was Bill who first understood as the second feather sliced through a policeman's back and exited his chest. "They're launching fucking arrows."

Screams masked the sirens, and *still* Ares continued forward as the dead piled up behind him.

When he reached the front door? Why, he simply opened it and stepped inside, lost from sight.

CHAPTER EIGHT

"All students and professors report to Viewing Hall B. This is Dean Pritcham. I repeat, all students and professors report to Viewing Hall B."

The words boomed from the ceiling, causing Dr. Byron to immediately stop talking. Claire raised an eyebrow as she stared at her favorite professor.

A student on the first row blurted, "Where's that?"

Dr. Bryon put his hands on his hips and looked quizzically as the speaker. "I'm not sure, to be truthful."

No one stood up, but rather waited for Dr. Byron. In the beginning, Claire couldn't stand the old man. Now she counted him as a mentor and a close friend. She wasn't going to leave his class until he dismissed them, regardless of what came over the intercom.

The professor finally looked at the class and shrugged. "I suppose we better listen. Let's see if we can't go find this viewing room." All the students stood and began packing up, but none dared reach for the phones in their pockets. Everyone in Dr. Byron's classes knew that to have a phone on, even if silent, could result in a verbal lashing. Even breaking national news couldn't interrupt his lectures.

Unless the dean summons everyone, Claire thought as she slung her bag over her shoulder. She looked around and saw Dr. Byron already walking up the stairs to the exit. She knew the other students in this class, but she wasn't close to any of them, certainly not like she was with Jack and Marissa. She was definitely close to the professor, so she jogged up the steps to catch him.

"What do you think this is?" she whispered as the two reached the door.

Dr. Byron ignored the question but turned around and looked at the rest of the class, which was still packing up. "I'm heading out to find this Viewing Hall B now. If you're quick, you can follow me. If you're slow, you'll have to find it yourself. However, quick or slow, every one of you better be there, or your grade in this class will suffer."

A few said, "Yes, sir," even though Claire knew everyone was going to obey. Some might look at their cell phones once Dr. Byron was out of sight, but they'd all show up.

Dr. Byron pulled the classroom door open and stepped through, Claire quickly following him. "I know you hear me. What do you think is going on?"

He walked quickly, and Claire kept up easily. He looked at her. "Ms. Hinterland, do you think I have a chip in my head?"

Claire deadpanned, "Like a potato chip?"

Dr. Byron rolled his eyes as they turned a corner. "Funny, Ms. Hinterland. Very funny. I have no more idea what is going on than you do; thus I'm trying to find Viewing Hall B." Up ahead, a group of students turned into the hall. "Ah, we must be heading in the right direction since the herd goes this way."

Claire shrugged. "Either that or to the slaughter."

Dr. Byron grinned a bit. "Your jokes are only *slightly* better than Mr. Teams'. How is he doing, by the way? I haven't seen him in a while."

Claire hadn't seen him since he and Marissa had dropped into her dorm room unexpectedly. She had done her best to *not* think about the things they'd said. "He's put on about twenty pounds of muscle, but other than that, he's the same Jack."

They turned into another corridor and saw open double doors, and above them was a sign that said Viewing Room B. "Not sure how I missed that for the past year," Dr. Byron commented. "Let's go see what this is about."

They walked in together. The lights were dimmed and a stage occupied the front of the room. Its stadium seating sloped downward. Claire was momentarily surprised she hadn't seen this room before, then she remembered everything *else* she'd seen in this building, and her surprise faded.

"Claire!"

She whipped her head around. Jack and Marissa were standing next to each other against the back wall, obviously waiting for her to get here. Claire turned to Dr. Byron, who was smiling. "Go on and sit with them. It was a shame they separated you three."

Claire smiled back and then trotted over to their corner. Sam was already there.

None of her friends were smiling. Jack's face was

solemn, and Marissa and Sam had tears in their eyes. Claire reached for Marissa's elbow. "What's wrong?"

Jack didn't respond, simply handed over his cell phone. Claire took it and glanced at the screen. He had a news website loaded, and the title said, *Attack on White House ends with President dead. Mythers responsible.*

"What...in...the actual *hell*?" Claire quickly scanned the article. There wasn't much of note, only that there were reports of a three-headed dog and birds that shot arrows from their bodies. She looked at Jack. "This has to be a joke."

He shook his head, taking his phone back. "Three-headed dog. We know who that is, and Marissa knows who the birds belong to."

Claire glanced at her friend.

"Ares, God of War," Marissa whispered.

Claire was about to respond when the double doors closed loudly. She watched Dean Pritcham as she took the stage.

"Thank you all for coming immediately." She stepped to the front, holding a microphone in her right hand. "Please, everyone, take a seat."

"Come on." Claire walked forward, automatically leading her crew although they technically *weren't* a crew—and they followed. The four sat on the far back left with Claire between Jack and Marissa and Sam on the other side of Jack.

The entire room fell silent as everyone took their seat. "I'm sure many of you heard the news already, but I thought it was best to gather everyone here. The United States of America is under attack, and from what the news is telling us right now, our President was murdered. While I can't confirm anything, and neither can the national news stations, it appears Congress is currently under siege."

The students gasped in unison. There were a lot more here than there had been last year, and many of them Claire didn't know. She looked around the darkened room and saw people holding their faces as they looked down and cried, some silently, some not. Marissa grabbed her hand, and Claire returned the grip.

Dean Pritcham raised the microphone again. "Right now, no one is sure who is to blame, but that isn't what concerns me. This university, and you students, are very valuable to this country, and protecting you is all that I am concerned about right now. Effectively immediately, all classes are canceled, and the university is being locked down. There will be no leaving the physical building, not even to go onto the grounds outside for the time being. I have contacted the FBI and am waiting to hear back from them. It's clear they're busy right now, but I am confident they will get back to me as soon as they possibly can."

Dean Pritcham paused, then walked to the far left side of the stage. She looked at the floor for a moment in silence.

"It's my judgment that being honest with you is the best policy I can adopt right now. Lying to you will not serve anyone. Some of you might be angry about not being able to leave. Some of you might be scared of what's happening. Those emotions are normal. All I ask is that you trust *me*. We will get through this, and I will update you as soon as I have more information."

She raised her head and looked at the group again.

"Professors, I'd like to meet with you directly after this assembly, so if you'll please remain when the students leave. Students, I know you have questions right now, but I won't be able to answer them since I don't have any answers to give. Please feel free to call your families and let them know you're okay, and trust that as soon as I know more, you will too. That's all. The students are dismissed."

Claire was stunned. She could see even from this distance how distressed Dean Pritcham looked.

"What the hell do we do?" Jack whispered.

Claire stood up. "Let's get out of the way and let them meet. That's probably the best thing we can do right now."

The other three stood and exited the row, entering the line to leave the room. Claire glanced at the professors as they stood up and moved toward the front of the auditorium. "No one's ever seen anything like this," she whispered. "No one has any idea how to fight it."

They left the auditorium without saying anything else. Claire caught glances from the rest of the students, perhaps wondering if the four of them would be able to do anything about the situation. Claire ignored it and kept quiet. She headed to her new dorm room without needing to tell the others where they were going. She waited until they were inside with the door shut before speaking.

"This isn't good." She leaned against the door and looked at her friends, who were finding seats.

Jack threw his legs up on her table. "'Isn't good' is when they only give you three shrimp in your lo mein. This is, like, end-of-the-world-type shit."

Claire glanced at Marissa, but her eyes had dried. She'd taken on a somber but not frightened expression.

Sam was sitting on the bed and staring at the opposite wall. "How many gods do you think they have over here now? How did they get Ares?"

Claire didn't have any answers so she shook her head in response.

Jack raised an eyebrow. "Where's Frank? You seen him or Al?"

Claire shook her head again. It seemed to be the only response she had right now. "I haven't seen Frank in a week or so, and Al for a lot longer than that."

Jack crossed his arms over his chest and leaned back in the chair. "You'd think Frank would show up for something like this."

Marissa flopped back on the bed. "It just happened. He hasn't had time to get here."

A knock on the door brought Claire out of her own head. Her face grew quizzical as she turned around to open it. She wasn't sure who would be coming to look for them right now, not about this. Certainly not the administration since the four of them hadn't trained as a group in months. She pulled the door open, and for an instant, she thought no one was there.

Then she felt a slight breeze as the ghost moved past her. "Howdy."

Jack shot up in his chair. "Al! Damn it, man, you're naked. Where are you?" The hair on Jack's head rose as Al blew on it.

"Right behind you, buddy."

Jack jumped all the way out of his chair, looking angry. "Cut it out! I almost pissed myself!"

The ghost chuckled, his voice resembling dead leaves

rolling over each other in the wind. For a moment, the excitement made Claire forget everything that had just happened. Only for a moment, though. "Where have you been?"

Jack didn't wait for an answer but walked over to Claire's closet. He threw open the door and started rummaging.

"What the hell are you doing?" she asked.

He pulled a shirt off its hanger. "Giving this dope some clothes. Put this on, Al. It's weird enough you having no body. At least let us know where you are." He held it in the air.

Al sighed and pulled it from his hands, talking as he did. "I've been in Boston for the past thirty-six hours. I was supposed to meet Frank yesterday, but he wasn't at the hotel he told me he'd be at. I hung around, thinking he was drunk or something at first, but then I started getting worried. I was downtown when I saw what happened and got here as quickly as possible. The city is frozen with fear right now, but it's going to thaw very quickly. I don't want to imagine what the people will do when that happens."

Claire stepped away from the door. "You don't know where Frank is?"

"No," Al responded. "And that's not like him."

Claire brought her right hand to her forehead. "That makes no sense, and combined with this, it's a bad omen."

"My thoughts exactly," the ghost said. "Sounds like Hades and Ares are to blame for what happened, and as bad as Hades is, Ares is a hundred times worse."

Marissa sat up. "It'll be okay, Claire. He can take care of himself, and the only time he's ever in danger is when the

FBI asks him to do something. They didn't do that since they're not using us right now. He's going to show up soon."

Claire shook her head. "No, Marissa, that's not true. They're not using *us* right now, but that doesn't mean they're not using Frank."

Jack sat back down in his seat, then leaned forward and placed his elbows on his knees. "What do you want to do?"

She gritted her teeth. "Find out what the hell is going on."

***

Claire didn't believe in coincidences, not after everything she'd seen. Frank could very well have been getting drunk somewhere, and indeed probably would have been—*if* this hadn't happened. But him being absent and the President being assassinated by two Greek gods?

Something was amiss.

So, she did what any stubborn-headed leader would do. She and her group marched down to the person in charge and knocked on her door.

Dr. Byron opened it, a wry smile forming on his lips as he did. "Why am I not surprised to see you four here?"

"There are actually five," she responded. "You just can't see one of 'em. Al is in the back."

Dr. Byron looked over his shoulder at the dean. "You want to let them in?"

Claire couldn't see Dean Pritcham, but she heard her sigh.

"I don't think they'll take no for an answer," was the response.

Dr. Byron turned back to the group. "Probably right." He opened the door wider, and Claire led the way in. She didn't sit down at her normal seat but stood behind it. Marissa and Jack took their usual spots, while Sam and Al stood next to Dr. Byron.

Dean Pritcham looked flat-out exhausted. "Can I help you, Claire?"

Claire put her hands on top of the wooden chair. "I'm not trying to cause you more grief right now, I promise, but I want to know what else you know besides what you told us. Frank is missing. Al was supposed to meet him a day and a half ago, and Frank never showed up, and now this. Those things are connected, and I'd like to know what's going on."

Dean Pritcham looked past Claire at Dr. Byron. She turned her palms up in the air, appearing exasperated. After a moment, she dropped her hands and gazed at Claire. "I wasn't lying in the auditorium. Everything I know, I told the group. The FBI still hasn't gotten back to me."

"Jack," Claire said without looking away from the dean, "what time is it?"

He glanced at his watch. "Five PM."

Claire raised an eyebrow. "It's been five hours, and you haven't heard from Lance or Remington? That in itself is weird, given that they wouldn't leave us alone for five minutes six months ago."

Dr. Byron spoke from behind her. "Claire, the President was just assassinated, and we still don't know how many congresspeople are dead. *That's* the reason they're not call-ing. It has nothing to do with Frank."

Claire looked over her shoulder. "Maybe that's true and maybe not. But Frank didn't meet Al, and it has something to do with this." She turned back to Dean Pritcham. "You really haven't heard anything?"

"No, Claire. Not a word."

Claire gripped the back of her chair until her knuckles turned white. She wasn't mad at anyone in this room. Indeed, she wasn't mad. She was *worried*. "And you called Remington?"

Dean Pritcham looked sympathetic as she nodded. "I promise that we are at nearly the top of their list. The moment they can contact us, they will, and I'll be sure to ask about Frank. Trust me, Claire. Right now, we're all we've got."

Claire took her hands away from the chair and shoved them in her pockets. The dean was right. They had to trust each other. "Let me know if you hear something, please. I'm sorry. You just know how I care about him."

Jack nodded. "How we all care about him. He's one of us."

Dr. Byron stepped to the door and opened it. "Okay, kiddos, the adults need to do some more talking."

Claire was the last to walk out, and Dr. Byron put his hand on her shoulder. "We're all in this together, Ms. Hinterland. Our enemy is the same. Don't forget that."

Dean Pritcham sat next to Dr. Byron, both of them looking at her laptop. They stared at the two familiar FBI agents, who looked even more tired than they did. It was three in the morning, and they were just now returning Pritcham's call. *I've never seen Remington and Lance look this awful,* she thought.

Remington spoke first. "Have either of you been watching TV?"

They both shook their heads, and Dean Pritcham answered, "No. Whatever it says won't be the full truth anyway. I waited to get it from you two, so don't bullshit me."

Lance sat forward in his wooden chair. Black bags filled the space under his eyes. "No bullshit. DC is on fire. Best we can tell, half of Congress was killed. Those ghosts we thought were staying put in Miami are moving now, heading toward the capital. There's mass rioting in the streets as well as unstable roads and subways as people try to exit all at once. The best information we have now is that the two Greek gods and their cult are holed up in the White House like tinpot dictators."

He leaned back in silence,

"Oh," Remington said. "There's also a forcefield around the place, so we can't get in there and kill them."

The dean was stunned, unable to find a word to say.

Dr. Byron reached forward and turned the screen slightly so he could see it better. "But they've hunkered down. They're not attacking anymore?"

Remington shrugged. "For now. The siege ended about an hour ago. Before that, it was seven creatures and a fucking dog waging war on the entire capital."

Dean Pritcham raised an eyebrow. "Seven?"

Remington sighed and closed his eyes, exhausted and without solutions. "Those cult members aren't as powerful as the gods, but each of them has some kind of power."

Dr. Byron glanced into the air as he thought. "We still don't know how they got those powers?"

The two FBI agents looked at each other for a brief moment, but Dean Pritcham caught it. "Hey, what was that? And don't say nothing because I saw it."

"It's classified," Remington responded.

"My ass, it is," the dean shot back. "I've got a school in lockdown over here and no clue what to do tomorrow, so first you're going to tell me what that look was about, and then you're going to tell me how we're going to protect these students."

The agents exchanged glances once again, then Lance rolled his eyes. "I guess it doesn't matter much at this point, and I'm honestly too tired to fight her. You want to tell her, or should I?"

Remington shook his head and looked at the camera. "We sent Frank through the Veil. We sent him home, and that's one of the things we asked him to look at—how they might have gotten their powers."

"Excuse me, gentlemen," Dr. Byron commented. "Can you say that again?"

Dr. Pritcham listened as the FBI agents explained what they had done, although neither of them knew *how* they'd done it. Either way, Frank was across the Veil, and in a few hours, they'd be attempting to bring him back. "You know she was in here asking about him?"

Lance's eyes narrowed. "Who?"

Dr. Pritcham's response was simple. "Claire."

Remington grabbed his tie's knot and loosened it, then undid his top button. "Why in God's name is she asking about Frank?"

"Apparently, he had a date with Al and missed it," Dr. Pritcham explained. "Now Claire is certain something is up, and I promised her I'd tell her what I found out."

Lance crossed his arms. "Yeah, you hear what we just said? This is classified information. You can't tell her anything, Dean Pritcham."

Dr. Byron put his hand on her arm, keeping her from the outburst she knew was about to erupt. "It's okay," he said. "The problem would be telling Claire before Frank is safe. She's asleep, I'm sure, or at the very least, it's too late to say anything. In the morning, when Frank is back, we'll let her know we've been in contact, and he's safe. That work for everyone?"

Remington dropped his eyes to his lap. "And if he's not back? If he's not safe?" He looked back up. "Because the truth is, we don't know if it's going to work. We're out on a limb here, and given everything that just happened, luck doesn't seem to be on our side."

Dean Pritcham was more thankful for Dr. Byron at that moment than she'd ever been. He was the calmest of everyone, a single ray of hope. "That's not how luck works, Agent Remington. You see, we've had a string of bad luck, so probability-wise, we should be getting some good luck right about now. Plus, while I can't see him in all his glory, Frank is a leprechaun, correct? They're known for good luck."

CHAPTER NINE

F rank coughed, and water spilled from his mouth and down his chin. He coughed harder, then rolled over on his side, and more water flowed from his throat.

"Zeus help me," he groaned as he opened his eyes. He didn't know where he was or what he was doing, only that his clothes and body were soaked. Also, the liquid in his mouth tasted salty instead of like hops.

He coughed again and threw up the last of it, water spewing onto the floor. He moaned as he pushed himself onto all fours and then to his knees.

Frank blinked three times. He looked to his left and right, then back at the being in front of him. "Am I dead?"

He wasn't sure who he was looking at, but he thought it might be who he wanted to see. The man was older and tall, with brown hair instead of gray. It was long and stretched down his back. His face was clean-shaven, and he sat on a throne that appeared to be made of...shells? They twisted and turned across the metal underpinning in beautiful blues and greens. A trident leaned against the throne.

Surrounding both the man and Frank was a transparent bubble-like structure. He had no idea what it was made out of, and didn't care, but outside it was water. Pitch-black water.

"You're not dead." The man's voice was deep and strong. "One of my servants saved you. Your kind and dwarves don't get along, so tell me, leprechaun, why did they bring you to my ocean?"

Oh, thank all the gods and fairies and even dwarves, it's him, Frank thought. *It's Poseidon, and somehow I'm in his castle at the bottom of the ocean.*

The god raised his eyebrows. "Do you hear me, leprechaun? You know who I am, don't you?"

Frank was still on his knees. He didn't want to explain it all again. "I imagine you're Poseidon, but the dwarves don't matter. They're just wannabe leprechauns. How much do you know about the Veil?" he asked without opening his eyes.

Frank understood that if this god wanted him dead, he would be dead. Even if he could teleport out of here, he'd end up outside the bubble beneath millions of pounds of pressure. His body would fold in on itself like an accordion.

"I've heard the rumors," the god whispered, but even that sounded full of power.

Frank put his hands in the air, palms out. He opened his eyes. "I don't have much time. Very soon now, I'm going to be pulled back to Earth or die, I'm not sure which and can't worry about it. I've got a story to tell, and then I need to ask for your help. An entire planet will be asking for your help."

The god's face was solemn. He placed both arms on the throne's armrests. "I didn't bring you here to kill you, leprechaun. Now tell this tale."

Frank dropped his hands and gave a half-chuckle. *All I ever wanted was a little beer and bowling. Instead, I had to steal that purse.* He started speaking.

───────

By the time Frank finished telling the story, he was lying on the floor and staring up at the ceiling. His skin had mostly dried, although his hair and clothing had a ways to go. He was silent for a while, waiting for Poseidon to say or do *something*.

Eventually, he tilted his head up and looked at the god. "Well?"

Poseidon wasn't looking at him, but appeared to be in contemplation, watching the black water outside. "There are a lot of powerful species. A lot of powerful creatures, too. I might be a king here, but there are other kings in other places who could rival my power if they wanted war. They probably speak other languages and have different body shapes, but there *are* other powerful creatures. What bothers me is, I'm not sure that in the entirety of creation there is anyone more cunning and conniving than my brother. Hades is gone, that is confirmed. I hear my nephew Ares is also missing, and with so many gods going missing..."

The god's hard eyes turned to Frank. "If Zeus isn't behind this, then I no longer deserve to have my kingdom because I can think of no one else who could create such a disaster and yet find a way to profit from it. How much time do you have, leprechaun, before the humans bring you back?"

Frank thought for a moment about telling him his name but discarded the notion. He let his head drop to the floor. "I have no idea. Not long. An hour maybe? Probably less."

Poseidon stood from his throne and began walking toward Frank. "And this girl, Claire—do you think she is worthy of fighting my family? Is she worthy of fighting gods?"

"Claire?" Frank chuckled. "Claire would fight the devil if she thought he was endangering her friends. She's as worthy as any creature I've ever met and twice as worthy as most."

The god now stood above Frank, staring down with dark eyes that spoke of powerful battles—in the past or future, Frank didn't know which.

"Good. Listen to me, leprechaun, and listen closely. Time is short, and you'll need to remember every word if you want to save Earth and your friends. Plus, I would rather sell my wife to a horde of dragons than let my brothers pull something over on me like this." He bent over so that his face was a foot or so from Frank's. "Can you listen well enough, green one?"

The leprechaun closed one eye as he stared upward. He didn't want to ask, but he just couldn't help it, so if it got him killed, he only wanted to half-see it coming. "Yeah, but I listen better with a beer in my hand. Ye don't happen to have any of those down here, do ye?"

CHAPTER TEN
A BRIEF PICTURE OF EARTH

While it was true that Hades had adopted the White House as his home, he was not resting or retired. Rather, the Underworld's god was doing two things simultaneously. The first and most annoying was keeping Ares from running outside to cause more havoc on the capital, although he hadn't been successful.

The second and most important was using the five humans he now considered his personal servants to mobilize their underground group. Across the globe, Mythers were appearing in massive numbers. They fell from the sky and rose from the ground. A huge octopus-like creature took down a tanker, wrapping an Empire-State-Building-sized tentacle around the middle and crunching it as if it were a potato chip.

In Egypt, it was reported that a horde of mummies one thousand strong rose from the sand and walked into Cairo. Guns were useful in putting them down, but not before many lives were lost in the terror.

The Ukraine saw a plague of zombies rise from their

graves. In that situation, guns were much less effective, at least until they immobilized the flesh-eating undead.

Loggers in a South American rainforest had been shutting down for the day, tired and ready to head back home. They heard leaves and twigs crunching around them, although they couldn't see what made the noise because of the brush. They thought at first some sort of predator cat had found them, but the creatures usually kept away because of the loud noises from the machinery. Each of the workers carried a submachine gun for this possibility. When the animals finally crossed the brush's barrier, they froze, unable to think much less fire their weapons. Staring at them were five velociraptors. When the first one launched at them, it was already too late for the men to even try to defend themselves.

Across America in cities large and small, boogeymen reached up from beneath beds and snatched children. Sometimes the kids made it out of the bedroom, but the boogeymen came out and marched down the halls to the parents' rooms. Some families made it. Others didn't.

Back at the White House, Hades was not pulling peaceful or neutral Mythers over. No, he wanted the dangerous ones.

Hour after hour, dangerous creatures flooded the Earth. They could be killed, although much havoc was wreaked upon people and buildings alike. The Royal Family of England woke up to a very different type of alarm clock as banshees flooded their halls, shrieking and knocking pictures off the walls. A quarter of the premises caught on fire when one of the banshees frightened a chef so bad he tried to use a crème brûlée torch as a flame thrower. The banshee survived, but the chef did not.

Leaders were summoned in every country. Some hid underground as they plotted and strategized. Others marched in the streets to show strength and solidarity, and at least one of those leaders died. When the enemy was in plain sight, militaries attacked. The strategies weren't coherent, and the tactics were mostly useless. This was an enemy that had never been seen in numbers, and often couldn't be seen at all.

The world was in a state of disaster.

And Hades was about to make it even worse because his ghosts had nearly reached Washington, DC.

CHAPTER ELEVEN

"**D**AMN THAT HURTS, YE BASTARDS!" Frank was hopping from one leg to the other, his whole body feeling like it had been electrocuted. He was in the same room he'd been in when he left, although it was now free of people. The black orb sat in the middle of the room like a lost relic. Frank finally quit hopping, wondering why it hadn't hurt the other two times he'd gone through the Veil, but this time his balls had nearly been burned off.

He turned to the one-way mirror. "Where are the two jackasses who brought me here? I need to talk to 'em and fast."

No one came through the door, but a voice spoke over an intercom above. "Hi, Frank. Agents Remington and Lance have been pulled away, but they'll be returning soon. We're going to ask you to wait in this building with us until they're able to do that."

Frank raised an eyebrow and smirked incredulously. "Is ye joking? This is some kind of a fucking joke, ain't it?"

Again the voice spoke from above. "No, Frank. I'm

sorry. Things have changed very drastically in the past two days, and we've had to change with them. I promise the agents will be back as soon as possible."

The door to the right opened and someone Frank had never seen before stepped through. The man appeared to be able to see Mythers because he didn't look at Frank in a strange way. "If you'll come with me, sir, I'd appreciate it."

Frank hadn't bargained for this. He put his hands on his hips. "And where exactly would we be going?"

"We're going to debrief in another room, sir," the man responded.

Frank pointed at him. "Debrief with ye? That's what ye planning on me doing?" He turned his head to the mirror. "Ye all better get on the horn with those two jackasses and tell them to Skype me or something, because I'm not debriefing with this ninny or anyone else. And if ye think ye can keep me here against my will, ye are in for a very rude awakening. That I promise ye." He gave the new guy his full attention. "Get to it, lad. Time's a wastin' we ain't got much to waste."

The man turned his head to the mirror and stared for a second, obviously unsure of what to do. He clearly hadn't expected to walk in here and find a leprechaun who wouldn't listen, let alone threatened violence. After a few moments, he walked out of the room and closed the door.

Frank looked at the mirror. "Ye better wise up and quick. We have a lot of things to do, and not much time to do it in. Also, someone either get me to a room with beer or bring it here."

Frank was pretty grumpy by the time Remington and Lance "showed up," which wasn't even accurate. Frank stood behind a chair with a desk in front of it, and on the wall was a flat-screen monitor that showed the FBI agents' faces. "Ye two think I'm going to debrief with ye like this? I didn't just almost die more times than I can count to talk to a television screen."

Frank was angry and stubborn, but he could see that Remington and Lance were stretched to their limits. They were paler than they'd been two days ago, the lines across their faces more pronounced, and both had bags beneath their eyes.

Frank placed his hands on the back of the chair. "Perhaps ye two should tell me what the hell happened here while I was gone?"

The agents put up no fight. They explained to Frank what had happened in DC, taking turns as they told the story and then describing what was taking place around the world. When they were finished, Frank circled the chair and sat down. The table was much too tall, so his head barely extended above it, but he didn't care. He needed to take a seat.

"So," Remington said, "We're in DC, strategizing with the Army and National Guard. We'd be there with you if we could, but right now, there isn't much choice in the matter. The entire world is focused on one problem right now, and we still can't solve it."

Frank nodded and didn't say anything. He'd never met Ares, although he'd heard of him—stories about him being a real asshole. Frank stared at the table as Remington asked his next question. "Did you learn anything over there? Anything that can help us?"

Frank nodded again, still trying to wrap his brain around what he had been told. "I think so, but it's going to be dangerous. And it involves Claire. I'm not sure how the FBI feels about that."

"Right now," Remington replied, "all options are on the table, so tell us."

Frank looked up, his face resolute. "No. I'm not going to tell you. I'm going to tell Claire, so there's no *miscommunication* about what is happening. Then, if she decides to do it, it's up to her. If you two want to be there, that's fine with me."

Remington combed his right hand through his short brown hair. "Frank, we really don't have the time or inclination to argue with you about this. What you're saying isn't in any protocol, and we can't get it approved."

Frank shrugged. "Well, that's a problem with yer protocol then, but it's not my problem. Plus, lads, ye know who I am. Do ye think you'll be able to keep me if I want to leave?" He shook his head. "No. I'll be out of here in two shakes of a lamb's tail and to Boston before ye two can find yer pricks to take a leak." He stood up and walked behind the chair. "Or we all can play nice, and ye two can hear what I have to say at the same time as Claire. It's up to you."

Lance rubbed his left eye, weariness obviously getting to him. "Why are you making this hard on us?"

"Not trying to, gents," Frank answered. "Simply need to do the best I can by me friends. So what's it going to be?"

Remington stood up and walked closer to the camera. "It's going to take us some time. We'll get back to you."

Frank's brow furrowed. He didn't like the sound of that. "And what would ye have me do until then? Wait in this room? I don't know if ye've looked around, but there's not a drop of golden amber to be found anywhere, nor a bowling ball as far as I can tell. This isn't somewhere I want to hang around in for a long time."

Now Remington rubbed his hand through his hair, roughly and multiple times. "You're giving me a damned headache, Frank, and that's the last thing I need right now. What the hell do you want?"

Frank grinned and winked at the agents. "That's what I like to hear. We need to focus on that more. What does Frank want? An airplane to Boston and a lot of beer for the ride. I'd like it within the hour, lads, because trust me when I say there's a lot to do and not much time to do it. Ye understand?"

"Just hold your damned horses, Frank," Remington said. "We'll be in touch." He reached forward and touched something on the camera. When the monitor went black, Frank was still standing behind the chair, alone in the room.

He didn't know if he'd made the right choice by refusing to tell the agents and saying he'd only give Claire the information. Time was short; he'd known that before he spoke with Poseidon, but after what he'd just heard? It was much shorter than he'd imagined, and by refusing to come clean, Frank had stretched the timeline out.

Either way, he needed to tell Claire this stuff personally, because while Remington and Lance might care for her, they cared more for their country. Frank didn't judge them for it. He just knew where his allegiance lay, and that was with her.

He looked around the bare room. *Those two better hurry up with the plane and beer because I'm not going to sit around here too much longer.* He walked over to the only door and twisted the handle. It didn't budge. There was a key card scanner to the side, and Frank had seen one on the outside as well. The door and locks didn't matter to Frank. He could teleport to the other side if he wanted to, but he was going to give them a little bit of time to talk to their bosses. He owed them that. If their bosses found out they'd lost the leprechaun who was supposed to help save humanity, it wouldn't be a great day for them.

Frank went to the far wall and laid down, placing his hands behind his head. He couldn't remember the last time he'd dozed, so a short nap wouldn't hurt. He'd only closed his eyes for a moment before he was in sleep's embrace.

"Frank, you are the laziest leprechaun I've ever met."

Frank's eyes jerked open wide.

"Get up, we've got to talk."

For a moment, he didn't know where he was or who was speaking to him. He leapt to his feet in a single bound, scanning the room for danger.

Then he saw the FBI agents on the monitor. He blinked a few times as his mind reminded him what was going on.

"How deeply were you sleeping?" Remington asked. "You look like you've got amnesia. Do you remember who I am?"

Frank blinked hard, clearing the sleep from his eyes. "Hush it, ye dope. I've been sitting in here waiting for ye to give me information for so long, I fell asleep. The world's burning and ye two are playing tiddlywinks with ye pricks. Now tell me what's going on."

It was the first smile either agents had produced in days, and it showed. There was the briefest amount of relief and hope, something instead of the drawn lines and worry. It only lasted a few moments, though. "There isn't time to bring everyone to Boston, Frank. Instead, we're going to bring Claire to the base of operations where you are, and we're going to meet her there."

That made sense to Frank. "Have ye talked to her yet?"

"No," Remington answered. "We wanted to talk to you first in case you decided to throw another wrench into the works. You're okay with her coming to you? Nothing else you need?"

Frank did a quick glance around the room. "I still don't see a single can of beer, lads. Tell me where that is, and I'll give me approval."

Lance sighed and looked at Remington. "We done here? I'm tired of the green man's jokes."

"Watch who you're calling a man," Frank demanded.

Remington nodded in response to Lance. "We're going to get in touch with Claire, and then we'll let you know what is going on."

Frank raised his palm into the air. "Hold on. Ye jokers can't keep me locked up the whole time. I don't even know where I am. Tell the lunkheads walking around this place to let me out and show me where the nearest bar is. Ye hear?"

Remington reached for the button on the side of the camera. "Maybe. We'll be in touch."

The screen went dark, and Frank was once again alone in this stupid room. "To hell with it," he said. If they weren't going to let him out, he'd go search for beer on his own. He walked to the door, and a bright light flashed. When it faded, the leprechaun was gone.

CHAPTER TWELVE

Claire listened to Dean Pritcham, but she wasn't quite able to believe what she was hearing. It was only her and the dean in the office, and she had come to get Claire personally. That was a first, and it showed how serious the matter was. Now, after listening to the dean speak for the past five minutes, Claire was wondering if the woman hadn't perhaps had an aneurysm during the past twelve hours.

"Dean Pritcham, I don't mean to be rude, but what you're saying is impossible. The FBI sent Frank to the other side of the Veil and then brought him back. No one has the technology to do that."

Dean Pritcham was patient, although obviously tired. "I don't know how it works, Claire. That's not my job, although nowadays, I don't really know what my job is anymore." She shook her head to clear that line of thought. "Regardless, the FBI wants to bring you to a small base of operations just outside DC. From what they've told me, Frank is there, and he won't talk to anyone but you."

Claire's instinct for not trusting people had grown razor-sharp over the past year. "Why wouldn't Frank just come here on his own?"

The dean crossed her hands as they lay on the desk. She took a few seconds before responding, obviously trying to figure out the right thing to say. Eventually, she said, "I understand why you would ask that question, Claire. I really do. You see the world as dangerous now, and you understand most of it isn't black and white. Or maybe it's that there is black and white for you, but in your mind, other people see things as gray, and that's where the danger lies. I don't know whether you're right or wrong."

She paused for a moment and took her eyes off Claire to glance out the window.

"I tried to anticipate the questions you would ask because everyone inside this thing knows how you are at this point. That's not a judgment, it's the truth." She brought her eyes back to Claire. "I'm not going to go through all the machinations with you. Maybe we have the time, and maybe we don't; I'm not concerned with it. The rest of the world might be gray, but you're going to have to trust me. Frank is waiting for you outside of DC, and we need to go so he can tell you something. I don't know what it is. I don't know if they'll even tell me what it is once I'm there. But if you want to assist with what's happening now, then that's what we do."

Claire hadn't said anything in a bit. She was taking it all in, and trying to balance her mistrust of institutional objectives with her place in them. Like it or not, at this point, she was a leader. Claire looked down at her jeans. "Okay, I'll go, but I'm bringing the group with me."

"That's fine," Dean Pritcham agreed, sounding relieved.

Claire raised her head. "It is?"

The dean was smiling. "We knew you were going to request that. They can go, except for Sam. Now—"

Claire gripped the sides of her chair. "Why can't Sam?"

"That wasn't my decision," the dean responded.

"Why can't she go?" Claire pressed.

She sighed. "There are quite a few reasons. She hasn't trained nearly as long as you three, nor has she been in as many dangerous situations. It would be irresponsible to put her in the field right now. And before you say anything, yes, it was irresponsible to do it last time. Both agents were reprimanded for that recommendation. More, it didn't work when we tried. She simply isn't prepared enough, and regardless of what happens going forward, we've all made a decision to not put any of you in unnecessary danger."

The dean paused for a moment, then tapped her finger hard on the desk. "As a leader, Claire, you should respect that. You know the difference between what the three of you have gone through and what Sam's been through. Having her along with whatever happens from here on out will make things more dangerous for everyone."

Claire was quiet for a few moments, but in the end, she knew the dean was right. "Fine. What about Dr. Byron? Can he at least come up there to hear what Frank has to say?"

Pritcham's brow furrowed.

"Didn't know I was going to ask that, did you?" Claire smirked.

The dean leaned back in her chair. "As an advisor?"

Claire rolled her eyes. "I mean, Dr. Byron isn't going out into the field with us. Yes, Dean Pritcham. We all respect his opinion, and I want to hear what he thinks about all of this if Frank really did make it across the Veil."

"I can't say for sure whether that's going to happen or not. It's fine by me, but the FBI and Dr. Byron will both need to sign off on it." Dean Pritcham stood up, and Claire followed suit. "Now, you go get the other students and let them know what's happening. You and they are not to tell anyone else. I'll handle the information about you being gone."

"Yes, ma'am," Claire responded. "When are we meeting back up?"

"You've got one hour to pack your things and get back here."

Claire knew how short that was, especially since she had to tell Jack that Sam wasn't coming. She said nothing else to the dean, simply fled the office.

CHAPTER THIRTEEN

Things went a lot easier than they could have, and Claire was glad for it. She'd told Jack and Marissa the plan, and also the limits placed on Sam. Jack had argued about it for a few minutes, but he saw reason quickly enough. He really did care about her and knew that she would be at more risk than the rest of them. Claire left it to Jack to deliver the news to her. When he came back, he looked like he'd just finished fighting a bear.

Neither Marissa nor Claire said anything.

The plane was waiting, and the four boarded—Dr. Byron had gotten approval and agreed to go. The ride only lasted a few hours, and Claire was quiet for most of it. Jack told a few lame jokes, but even he couldn't find the energy to make a real effort.

The world had just changed in a very drastic way. Claire didn't know if Hoaxers still existed now that the United States' capital was overrun, but she thought they would be in the fringe if so.

More, what was she supposed to do there? Claire

Hinterland from a tiny town, who'd barely been able to squeeze through the encounters she'd had with Mythers already. Each time she'd been able to do it because she had help, not to mention a pretty powerful Myther in Frank as well. Now they were calling her to the capital, and for what? Claire had thought over and over about her fight with Hades, and she didn't know if she'd won. She wouldn't be able to replicate it, and from what she could tell, that Ares bastard was even more dangerous.

If the United States government was expecting her to save the world, they were making a serious mistake. She and her friends weren't saviors. They were little more than kids, and this entire endeavor had been stupid from the outset. Maybe on paper it looked like it might work, but in reality?

Claire decided to try to get some sleep. She would go hear what Frank had to say, but most likely, she and her group would fly right back to school. Dr. Pritcham was right—there wasn't any need to put more lives in danger.

Frank didn't like the looks of this group or this room, which was larger than any he'd sat in with this group of people. There were at least four cameras in it that he could see. A long rectangular table occupied the middle of it, although there were at least ten feet of space from it to the walls. A set of double doors allowed entry and exit. Frank sat on the far side of the table in front of those doors and watched his friends and the FBI pile in.

Remington and Lance gave him nasty glares. Frank

smiled, grabbed the mug of beer in front of him, and tipped it toward them. He'd been on a drinking binge and was as close to tipsy as he'd ever been. Learning about Ares and Hades... Perhaps he was coping with it. He wasn't sure, but he was frightened.

Get it together, ye old green idiot. Look at them right there. Herself looks like she's holding the weight of the world on her shoulders, and ye haven't even told her what ye need from her. If ye don't at least look a bit peppy. Frank grabbed his beer and took a large sip from it as the crew found their seats. He let out a five-second belch when he was finished.

He looked at the two FBI people he didn't know—a man and a woman, at the end of the table—and grinned widely. "Top 'o the morning to ye both."

The agents said nothing, only pulled legal pads from their bags.

"Friendly ones, they are," Frank said as he turned to the six in front of him. Claire sat next to him, with Jack and Marissa flanking them. Remington and Lance were on the far right, with the professor taking up the left side. "Hey, prof, can ye see me yet?"

Dr. Byron leaned back in his chair and studied Frank for a moment. "I see more of you than last time. Your skin seems to be a darker tint, but I can't make out what it is."

Frank waved away the comment. "Nobody's perfect." He turned to Remington. "I don't know those two on the far end, but when I run out of beer, I expect either ye or them to get it."

Remington looked at the people on his right. "Frank disappeared for the past ten hours and got about as close to drunk as I've ever seen him. We might arrest him when this is all over; that hasn't been decided yet. However, I apologize for his current state." Remington nodded at the two people at the end of the table. "We're going to keep their names quiet for now, but they're here to observe. They won't be asking any questions, only detailing what is said here."

Frank pointed at two of the cameras on the far side of the room. "What about those? Aren't they good enough to observe? I'm sure ye got a whole team of FBI spooks watching us."

Remington ignored the question and focused on Claire's group. "You know what happened with Frank. We asked to debrief with him alone, but he refused without you being present." He turned back to Frank. "Now, without further ado, will you please tell us what the hell happened over there?"

Frank shook his head in mock disappointment and looked at Claire. "Do ye see how they treat me? After all I've done for them."

"Frank," Claire responded with anger in her voice, "we need to get serious. Please."

Frank gave her his most charming grin while thinking, *I have to play the game, lass. If not for you, then for the two with ye.* "Okay, okay. I'll calm it down for ye, Claire, although I reserve the right to complain about me unfair treatment in the future." His smile faded, although he tried to be conscious of how serious he grew. "Since I left, ye have let the world go to hell, apparently. I did get some good information while I was away, though. First, I know who's behind the Veil tearing. Second, I know what they're scared of. Third, I know how those five peasants got the powers. And lastly, I know how to get ye three the same."

Remington dropped his pencil on the desk. "We're not going to play Twenty Questions with you, Frank. Tell us what you know."

Frank rolled his eyes and grabbed his mug of beer. "Don't get ye panties wadded up, lad. Just wetting me whistle." He took a long sip. "Ahhh. First, Zeus is behind the whole thing. Second, he's scared of ye, Claire." He pointed at her.

Claire jerked back in her chair. "Me? That's impossible, Frank. Why?"

Frank shook his head, bewildered. "Those gods, lass. They're superstitious folk. I imagine an oracle told him, but who can say for certain? Either way, he believes you're the one meant to stop him." He pointed a thumb at himself. "Me personally? I think the gods are seriously discounting old Frank's contribution, and I don't think ye have a snowball's chance in hell, but that's just me."

He shot Claire a wink, and she glared back.

Frank shrugged. "I really don't know. That's just what the god thinks, and that's why a lot of this is playing out as it has. He thinks you can defeat him. Be that as it may, he also called those twerps over to the other side—the five that are following Hades around like lapdogs. That was where they got their powers. Zeus endowed them."

Claire turned to her right to look at Marissa and Dr. Byron. "Can he do that?"

Dr. Byron nodded while Marissa spoke. "Yes, according to the stories. He could change people's shape and give gods and humans powers. It's a thing."

Frank nodded in Marissa's direction. "Listen to the lass. It's a thing. Now, that's where they got their powers, and although we have that English doc down there making gadgets, he's not going to create anything strong enough to face Ares."

Claire raised a hand to stop him. "Ares is stronger than Zeus? That's what you're telling me?"

Frank leaned back in his chair and rubbed his index finger down the side of his glass as he thought. "More powerful? No. I'm not sure there are any gods more powerful than Zeus, not if you include how conniving he is. Ares is *dangerous*. Zeus would never try to fight him one on one because Ares is out of his damned mind. He's arrogant, cruel, and probably a psychopath. Zeus wanted him over here first so he'd kill you, then Zeus could skip on over and pick up the pieces." Frank snapped his fingers. "Quit interrupting me, lass. I'm losing me way. I was saying, if ye want to have any chance of stopping those two and Zeus, yer going to need some powers yerself."

Jack smiled. "Powers, Frank? What kind of powers?"

"All these questions," Frank grumbled. "Just hold them until the end. Now, through me courage, heart, and brains, I was able to find someone who will help us. We can get ye endowed with powers, but it's not going to be easy. Truth be told, ye will probably die doing it. However, that's what I was able to find out." Frank stopped talking and took another long sip of his beer. He didn't want to tell them the plan because of how ridiculous it sounded. Maybe if he just drank his beer and hid behind the mug, they'd leave him alone.

"Well," Claire said, "what is it? How do we get our powers?"

Frank groaned as he set his beer down. "Always with the questions." He looked down at the table. "You heard of Prometheus?"

Jack said, "Why don't you remind me?"

Dr. Byron gave him a harsh glare. "You should know who he is since it was in your syllabus."

Jack leaned away from the professor. "I know who he is, Dr. Bryon. I just need a *gentle* reminder."

Marissa sighed. "He is a Greek titan who defied the gods. He brought humanity fire and helped create civilization in the stories. Zeus punished him by tying him to a rock and having an eagle eat his liver every day, only to have the liver grow back each morning. In one of the legends, someone freed him, although I'm not really sure who that was right now."

Frank frowned, nodding. "That's pretty much right on our side, but I don't think he got punished for bringing fire to *humans*. It was something similar, but Zeus did tie him to a rock. Either way, he'll help us if we can get to him. He'll give us powers to try to stop Ares."

Lance spoke from the far right side. "Can you bring him here? Is that what you mean?"

Frank choked on his laugh. He started coughing, and it took him a moment to settle. "Bring the Titan that Zeus hates to Earth? Is that what ye said? Sure, I don't think he'll have any problem coming out of hiding to jump across a Veil and risk torture forever and ever, amen. Yer mad, ye know that, Lance? Mad." He shook his head and looked at Claire. "It's up to ye, lass. If ye want to go over there and search for power, then we'll go. If ye don't, then we won't." He leaned back in his chair, having said everything he needed to say. It was out of his hands.

Remington stood up. "With all due respect to everyone in this room, the decision isn't up to Claire. We appreciate you all coming here. We're going to ask that you stay for another few days while we discuss our options."

Frank had known that was coming, but the people on the other side of the table apparently did not. Jack leaned back in his chair and looked at the agents. "What the hell do you mean, you appreciate us coming here? If he says we have a way to fight those gods, we're gonna take it."

Frank was proud of Jack. He'd changed from the boy Frank had met a year ago. He wondered if Claire saw it too. If Claire knew how much she'd done to help mold him.

Lance didn't stand up, but rather looked at Frank. "Are we able to send someone else?"

"Nope. The person I spoke to thinks she's the one who has the best shot, so she's the one he'll help take."

Remington turned back to the table. "You didn't speak to Prometheus?"

Frank's eyes grew wide. "Are ye mad, man? I have no desire to die. No, I didn't speak to a god who's in hiding. I spoke to Poseidon, Zeus' brother. He's the one who's going to help us with passage, but he's not going to do it for anyone besides Claire."

Remington looked at the strangers on the other side of the table. "I'm going to take them to their rooms for now. Get more details out of Frank, and we'll come back to debrief."

"Oh, now they can talk?" Frank tapped his mug on the table as he looked at the new agents. "Ye want to chat, yer going to give me a refill."

Frank kept his eyes on Claire as she stood, ready to follow the agents out of the room. *What are ye thinking, lass? Ye surely didn't tell us here.*

CHAPTER FOURTEEN

Hades understood that he couldn't keep Ares locked up in this building forever. Sooner or later, the god would stop listening to him and leave. Two days had passed, and while the humans continued trying to destroy the building and those now residing in it, they were having no luck. Yet, the girl hadn't returned. None of the students had.

Hades had called his little crew into one of the infinite rooms in this place. Ares showed up, probably more from boredom than anything else. He leaned against the door and was meticulously checking his fingernails.

The five humans stood in front of Hades, who started pacing in front of them. "I'm going to ask questions," he told them, "and I don't want your normal bumbling, fearful garbage. I want straight answers, and I want them fast. In fact..." He stopped pacing and turned to the five. "One of you is going to be the designated answerer. If you bumble, you die. Fred, you're starting."

Fred's eyes widened, but he made no other movement.

"Good." Hades started pacing again. "Now, why haven't they arrived? Those kids and that girl. Where are they?"

Fred swallowed hard before opening his mouth. "I'm not sure. The world might think this attack is too big for them to handle."

Hades shook his head as he walked. "That doesn't make sense. She is the prophesied one who can stop all this. Why won't they allow her to come?"

Fred glanced quickly at his comrades but must have remembered what would happen if he bumbled. "Earth doesn't believe in prophecies, at least not modern-day ones. They won't see her as a savior, but only as a kid. Most likely, if they haven't sent her by now, they're not going to."

Hades stopped walking. "Why didn't anyone mention this before? That I would come here and create such a spectacle that it would keep humanity from sending the girl?"

Fred was sweating now, large beads rolling down his forehead. A ring of dark liquid was soaking into his collar, too. "We didn't know. You're asking me what I think *now,* and this is the best answer I have. They think this is too big of a problem for her or that college. None of us could have predicted they would think that."

Hades walked over to the nearest chair and collapsed into it, then brought his right hand to his forehead and lightly rubbed it. "Then how do I get the girl to come here?"

Ares' voice boomed across the room. "Let me go outside. If the spectacle is too big for her now, the only correct course of action is to create an even bigger spectacle—one that forces them to consider things they wouldn't have before. If you want her to come, this mythical girl of supreme status..." He chuckled. "Let me go outside. I'll get her here, dear uncle."

Hades continued rubbing his forehead. Perhaps Ares was right. Sitting in here blocking air- and tank strikes wasn't bringing Hades any closer to his goal. Not to mention, he also had to consider what Zeus was doing on the other side. How much did he know, and when would he decide to step across?

Action was better than complacency.

Hades put his hand in his lap and looked up. "What do you want to do?"

Ares pushed himself off the door, standing up to his full height. "Just let me go to war. She'll come when I'm finished."

Jack burst into Claire's room with Marissa following right behind. "Turn on the television *now*."

Claire had been reading on her bed for the past eight hours. She didn't want to watch television because there wasn't going to be anything good on. She already knew everything they were talking about, one way or another, and it all centered on doom.

She sat up, closing one of the books that Dr. Byron had given her to read—*The Rebellious Sister*. "Why? What's going on?"

Jack didn't waste time talking. Their rooms were like a

college dorm room, only more military-looking, but each had a small television on a desk. He went to it, pressed the on button, and cycled through the channels until he found a news station.

Claire's book dropped into her lap. Jack and Marissa stood on opposite sides of the television, staring at it.

It wasn't an anchor from a news station recording it. Someone was using their phone and was entirely too close for safety, but there all the same. A man Claire had never seen before stood in the middle of the road. Two tanks were about twenty feet away from him on either side. Something was on fire just outside the camera's view, so she couldn't see what was burning.

"Is that him?" she whispered.

Jack shook his head. "Hell if I know, but they've been showing this for about five minutes. Watch! Watch!"

A soldier popped up from the top of the left tank. The man—Ares, probably—turned to face him. The soldier held a gun the size of those they showed in the films, and he started firing at once. The bullets rained down on Ares and the surrounding area. Huge chunks of pavement exploded into the air, turning to dust, pebbles, and rocks. Claire stared at the god, her mouth agape. There was damage all around him, but nothing had harmed him.

"My God," Marissa whispered.

Claire knew exactly what she meant. The sheer power of that gun was breathtaking, yet it couldn't even *touch* this god. The bullets shattered when they hit his body, exploding into dust particles.

Ares began walking, his steps almost leisurely. His face was turned upward toward the soldier. He raised his right arm as he stepped forward, and in one motion, he pulled a spear off his back and flung it. It was like a bolt of lightning rushing through the air, hardly noticeable until you saw what it struck. The soldier fell backward but not out of the tank, the spear having hit the only part of his body not fully protected—his neck.

Marissa brought her hands to her mouth.

The tank started rolling forward, obviously unsure of what to do but hoping to crush the god under its treads. Someone dragged the man's body inside the vehicle, then more deadly bullets flew from the tank, doing no damage to Ares.

Jack took a step back from the television. "He's like Superman."

Ares reached the tank and leapt onto the top in one bound. The jump was easily twenty feet, but he'd made it look like a single step. The gunner quit firing and the tank stopped rolling since they couldn't see their enemy. Ares grabbed the hatch and ripped the metal cover off. Bullets flew through it and Ares leaned back for a moment, letting them soar into the air.

Then, he hopped into the tank and was gone from view.

Claire could hear muffled gunshots inside, but as the seconds passed, it died down until there was nothing.

"What in the hell is happening?" Jack whispered.

Claire didn't respond, simply watched and waited.

The tank's main gun moved about a foot over, and then she understood as surely as the other tank did what was happening. The other crew didn't react quickly enough, but the cannon fired, its payload smashing into the opposite tank. The metal vehicle nearly split in two, and fire roared into the sky.

Claire stepped forward almost unconsciously and turned the television off. No one said anything to her about it. They all stared silently at the TV.

"This..." Claire's voice trailed off. "This changes things."

Jack shook his head. "How?"

"I hadn't seen what he could do before. I hadn't watched the news because there wasn't anything I could do. I knew it would be bad, but this is the first time I've witnessed his power." She stared at the television in silence for a moment. "Hades was strong, but he wasn't a warrior. This god is."

"What does that change?" Jack asked.

Claire looked him in the eyes. "I'm going across the Veil to get whatever power I can find and bringing it back here to kill this bastard."

When Claire left her room, she didn't have a clue where she was heading. This underground bunker was top secret and large. The hallways were maze-like, but she knew if she walked long enough, someone would find her. That was what she was hoping for. She hadn't bothered to grab Dr. Byron from his room because she didn't want his input. Her mind was made up, her spine having turned to steel again.

Finally, two men had appeared at the end of a hallway—not Remington or Lance, but wearing similar suits.

There'd been some arguing, some curse words, and

finally, they'd brought the three to the room Frank was in as a compromise, since she'd demanded to see Remington and Lance immediately. The agents probably could have used force to do what they wanted—or at least tried—but they knew who the kids were and their value to the world. Using force on them would have been worse than letting them wander freely or putting them with the leprechaun.

Claire wasn't happy when they were locked in the room with Frank, but she knew it would get Remington and Lance back quicker—or at least get their attention.

Jack sighed at one point and said, "I wish I had a watch. Never thought I'd need one." The FBI had taken his phone before letting him enter the building.

Claire was mostly quiet as they waited, except for a brief interaction with Frank. "You've never seen him? Ares?"

The leprechaun was lying on top of the table, his hands beneath his head and his legs crossed. "No, lass. Only heard stories, as one does."

Claire was sitting in the corner, her knees pulled up and her arms resting on them. "He's tougher than anyone I've ever seen. How tough a task is it to get those powers?"

Frank tapped his toes together for a moment, then said, "Probably a bit like crawling through ten miles of glass."

Jack laughed. "Well, thanks for being honest with us."

"Not a problem, lad," Frank responded. "Frank is always looking out for ye."

Claire's face was like granite. "That's fine. We'll crawl those ten miles. How powerful is it going to make us?"

Frank pulled his hands out from behind his head and rested them on his stomach. He was silent for a bit. "That's a hard question, lass. Magic or power largely depends on the user, from what I understand. Take dwarves. They can't handle the power of teleportation, which is why they don't have it. Vampires are a stronger lot, though no less digusting—"

Marissa interrupted. "Frank, has anyone ever told you you're a racist?"

Frank raised a finger. "One, these are species. Two, no, because I'm not. Did ye like the vampires we met? I think not. And when ye meet a dwarf, ye will think the same." He put his hand back down. "Now, please quit being rude and interrupting me. Power won't flow to those who aren't strong enough to handle it, 'least that's me understanding. So Prometheus will grant us what we can wield, and obviously, I will wield the most due to me strength. It will cascade down from there, with Claire holding the least of all of us." Frank grinned as he finished the last bit.

Jack had been sitting against the wall but laid on the floor. "So, Ares is like super strong? His underlying...I don't know, architecture or whatever?"

Frank shook his head and narrowed his eyes as he thought. "I'm not sure, lad. He's a god, and things are a bit different for them than us mere mortals."

Claire had let the conversation go, having heard what she wanted. Coming up here, she hadn't thought she could be of any use. When she'd left the first debriefing, she hadn't said anything, wanting to keep it to herself. Then she'd decided she wasn't sure what her small group could do against someone who'd wiped out the whole government, but she would be willing to try. She would have gone across the Veil if the FBI had let her. For her family and friends, she was willing to try.

After seeing the tank massacre? There was no way she would let that creature go unchecked. She would die first.

Eventually, Remington and Lance arrived. Their ties were undone, and they looked even more tired if that was possible. Remington closed the door and looked at Claire, who was still sitting in the corner. " I wish I never met you. Your annoyance factor is reaching the point that it might be costing lives by having us come down here."

Claire stood up. "I didn't recruit you. What did the powers that be say? They letting us go over there?"

Lance stepped away from Remington and moved to the head of the table. He pulled the chair out and leaned on the table with his hands, then stared directly at Claire. "You've been quiet about everything up until this little tantrum. Do you *want* to go?"

"That's what this tantrum is about. I'm going one way or another, but if I have your permission, it'll probably be best for everyone."

Remington raised his right eyebrow, a small smirk on his lips. "Yeah? How do you plan on going without our help?"

Claire smiled. "I have more connections with Mythers than you do. I'm sure one of them can find a way, and if not? Well, I'll just have Frank here teleport Marissa and me to that orb and let Marissa use spells to make it work. One way or another, I'm going over there and getting whatever powers I can find."

Remington leaned against the door, still smirking. "To

be clear, I don't think you could do any of that. You could try, but you wouldn't get across."

He stopped talking, and Lance picked up the conversation. "However, with the way things stand now, the higher-ups have decided if you and your parents are both willing to sign off and risk it, they'll let you go."

Jack jumped to his feet. "What about us? Me and Marissa?"

Marissa shook her head. "It's Marissa and me."

Lance ignored the interruption. "Frank, you said you can't send anyone else. That they're only going to deal with Claire. If those other two go, will they be able to get powers too?"

Frank didn't move or sit up. He kept staring at the ceiling. "Yes, I did manage to throw their names into the bargain, because I know Claire can't handle this on her own." He grinned at the joke. "But to everyone who's involved with this except humans, Claire is the special one. They won't take a substitute."

Lance nodded at the answer, then looked at Jack, who was still on his feet. "We got permission for you two as well. No to Sam, and that's final."

Jack nodded. "That'll work."

"So," Remington started, "if you want to go, we're ready to move on this as soon as possible. You'll undoubtedly need to talk to your parents, and if they don't sign new papers, it's a no go."

Marissa stood up. "What are the papers?"

Lance took his hands from the table and straightened up. "You're all adults in the legal sense, but if this doesn't go the way we want it to, your parents need to be on record as having known and agreed."

"Covering yer ass," Frank commented.

Remington shrugged. "Whatever you want to call it is fine with us. That's the deal. You want to call your parents?"

Claire climbed to her feet. "Where's a phone?"

CHAPTER FIFTEEN

There'd been tough conversations with Claire's parents before but never like this. She'd been confident when she asked for a phone, but now as she looked at it, her confidence drained. It wasn't that she didn't *want* to go; that part hadn't changed one iota. It was that she didn't want to ask her parents' permission. She didn't want to ask them to say she could die for this war, because that was what they'd be doing.

Frank had made it back, yes, but did that mean they could do it again? More, would they even survive the trials to get the powers? There were so many questions and so many risks.

And she was about to ask them to let their only daughter run those risks.

They'll have to understand, she thought, *like I do, that there is more at risk here than me. Like them. Like Jack and Marissa and Dr. Byron. Like everyone I love.*

She picked the phone up and dialed their number.

After a few rings, her father picked up. "Hello?"

"Hey, Dad."

"Oh, God," he said, and he began weeping. She heard him yell into the other room, "Get on the phone! It's Claire!"

There was a rush of tears from both her parents, and then came the worries. She hadn't called. The university wouldn't put them through to her. The FBI wouldn't even take their calls. They didn't know what was happening.

"Are you okay?"

"Are you in danger?"

"Why haven't you called?"

Claire answered their questions patiently, letting them get the anxiety out of their systems. After about ten minutes, she was able to get to the reason for the call. "Mom, Dad, I've called to ask you something."

There was a pause on the line, then her father tentatively asked, "What is it?"

Claire closed her eyes, the phone pressed to her ear. "You've seen and heard what's happening, right?"

"Yes," her mother answered. "Why do you think we're so worried?"

Claire nodded on her end, understanding how hard this would be for them. "There's a chance I can stop it, but I'll need your approval."

"Absolutely—" her mother started.

Her dad interrupted her. "How could you stop it?"

Claire spoke in a rush and firmly. She told them about her first mission. She told them about the second one. She told them about the witches. She told them about Hades and the training. She told them about Frank, about him going and coming across the Veil. She told them about the plan, the possible acquisition of powers. And after all that, she told them the risk. Claire told them everything, and then she waited.

The pause was longer, even her mother not saying anything. Perhaps they were in the same room, and her father had given her a signal not to speak. Or maybe the magnitude of what she told them kept their words at bay.

"Honey," her father began, "I can't even begin to think about what you just said. We had no idea about any of that, and one day we're going to talk about you keeping it from us, although I know this isn't the time." He paused for a few moments. "What you're asking us... It was one thing to send you to the university before all this started. That was your future we were thinking about. It was a way out of this town. This..."

"It's suicide," her mother interjected, her voice reflecting the tears that were surely in her eyes.

Claire sighed. "It's not suicide, Mom. Did you hear everything I just told you? Did you hear everything we've already accomplished?"

Her mother's voice firmed up. "I saw that man today, the one with the tanks. I saw how bullets couldn't even stop him. I know that he killed our President, and I know *he* is in control of Washington, DC. Not *humans*. Him. So with all due respect, my daughter, you're asking our permission to get killed."

Claire's father said nothing, his silence tacit agreement with her mom.

Claire opened her eyes and stared at the phone. They had to say yes. That was all she really knew. If they didn't, Claire had no idea what the world would do. It sounded arrogant in her mind, but that was the truth. Their tanks couldn't hurt this god. Their missiles couldn't touch him. He was something beyond humanity, and to beat him, they would need help from beyond humanity.

"I don't understand what you're feeling," Claire said into the phone, "but I do understand what I'm asking. I wouldn't do it if I had another choice. I don't want this on my shoulders, but that's where it's fallen. If I don't go, there's no one else. I need you both to see that. If I don't go, the world most likely falls to those creatures."

Her mother's voice was nearly hysterical. "Let it fall then."

Claire shook her head. "If it falls, *you* fall. I fall. Everyone back home falls. This isn't something you can avoid, or I can avoid if we stick our heads in the sand. Either you agree to this or..." She sighed, pausing for a long moment. "Or I might as well come home and we'll start preparing to hide."

She heard her mother crying, but it faded as she stepped away.

"Your mom can't handle this right now," her dad whispered. "This is hard to ask me, but it's probably harder to ask a mother since she's the one who carried and bore you."

"I wouldn't ask if I had any other choice."

"I think your mom knows that," her dad said. "That was why she left. She can't handle it because she loves you so much."

Claire didn't know what else to say. All she knew was time was short. "Are you going to give me your blessing?"

She heard her father pull a chair out at the kitchen table and imagined him sitting down. "I don't think we have much choice, from how you make this sound. You're sure, Claire? Positive that no one else can do anything? You're the only one?"

Claire thumped the small table in front of her, tears forming in her eyes. She hated doing this, but they were out of options. "I'm sure, Dad. If there was anyone else, I wouldn't be asking you."

Her father's voice cracked as he spoke. "I love you, Claire. Since the moment I laid eyes on you, I've loved you with all my heart. You know that, right?"

Claire closed her eyes, and a tear spilled from the corner. "I love you too."

"When are you going?" her father asked, obviously trying to hold back a flood of tears.

"As soon as we get the signatures."

"Okay." Her father breathed huskily into the phone as if he were about to break down. "You think you can make it back?"

Claire grinned through the tears flowing down her face. "I think I have to. Mom sounds like she's about to have a stroke, and I can't have that on my conscience."

Her dad managed a chuckle. "You come back to us, Claire. We need you. Get me the papers, and we'll sign them. I'll take care of your mother for now, but when you get back, you're taking a break from school and coming down here."

Claire knew her father was acting as if she didn't have

to battle a god when she returned, but that was fine. They'd ignore that for now if it made this conversation easier. "Okay, Dad. Stay by the phone, and someone will be in very shortly. I love you, and you tell Mom that I love her too. So much. I'm coming back."

"You promise?"

Claire finally opened her eyes. "I promise."

CHAPTER SIXTEEN

"That sucked," Jack said as the group walked down the hall. "I didn't think I'd be able to get them to agree. It took me about two hours."

"What about you, Marissa?" Claire asked.

The conversation with her parents was obviously weighing on Marissa. Her face was the perfect picture of sadness. "Same. I'm honestly not sure they're going to sign."

The group turned right. "They said they would, right?" Claire asked.

Marissa nodded solemnly. "Yeah, but with the way they sounded, they might change their minds. I don't know."

All three had told their FBI handlers that their parents agreed, and now they were heading to the conference room, as Claire was coming to think of it. They weren't sure how long it would take for everything to be signed, but they figured they'd hang out with Frank for a while and see what answers they could get out of him regarding the other side of the Veil.

They reached the room and Claire opened the door,

expecting to see Frank lying on the table again. She thought he didn't have a room like theirs as punishment for escaping before, although he could readily escape again if he wanted to.

Frank wasn't lying on the table but sitting at the very end, his feet up on it. He had a can of beer now, and a case sat right in the middle of the table. Behind it was Dr. Byron with an open beer in his hand.

"I was beginning to think you had forgotten I'd come."

Claire opened her mouth to say something, but she realized she *had* forgotten. Jack pushed past her and started talking. "You know, Dr. Byron, Claire did forget all about you, but I didn't. We were walking down the hall just now, and I said we need to go speak with our esteemed professor as soon as possible. I'm so glad you're here."

He grabbed a chair and sat down, grinning wildly.

Claire moved into the room, Marissa following. "I'm so sorry, Dr. Byron. I just—"

Dr. Byron waved her comments away with his free hand. "I didn't get this old by being stupid, Ms. Hinterland. Frank here has been generous enough to tell me what's going on, and I understand that your professor probably wasn't at the top of your mind."

Jack rapped his knuckles on the table. "Top of *her* mind. Me? You're always on my mind, Dr. Byron."

The professor took a sip of his beer with one mistrusting eyebrow raised. "I'm going to need to get a restraining order if that's the case." He turned his attention back to Claire and Marissa. "Please, you two sit down. From what I understand, we have some time until the FBI has all their papers signed."

Claire shook her head, angry with herself for having been so selfish. She went to the left of Jack and took a seat. Marissa sat down next to her.

Frank put his beer on the table. "Good to see ye too. No one wants Frank anymore. It's like I'm chopped liver."

Claire chuckled. "Sorry, Frank. How are you?"

Frank turned his head up to the ceiling. "Bored. I could get out of here if I wanted to, but I know ye all are going to be in for a tough time once we get over there, so I'm sticking around. But I'm bored."

Jack threw his legs up on the table too. "I agree, Frank. You and me, we're sophisticated creatures. The end of the world doesn't interest us. We prefer fine wine and fine women."

Claire gave him a look. "I'll be sure to tell Sam that."

Jack's eyes widened, and he shook his head quickly. "No, no. No need for that."

Dr. Byron set his beer on the table and gently pushed it away from him. "Okay, okay. As much as I like you all, I don't enjoy hanging out with you as much as you might think. I'm here for a reason, as I'm sure you've guessed."

Jack raised a hand as if in class. "To impart wisdom to us?"

Dr. Byron stared at him for a moment. "I'm a professor. That is my entire purpose for being in your life. So yes, you are right. Someone give him a cookie."

Jack put his hand down, smiling, obviously enjoying the banter. Dr. Byron rolled his eyes before continuing. "What is being asked of you? You might think it's strange or insane. You're not even out of your teens yet, and grown-ups are asking you to save the world."

Jack was about to say something smart, but Claire elbowed him.

"Thank you, Ms. Hinterland," Dr. Byron said. "What I wanted to tell you all is that no one is asking you to do anything that they haven't asked of the generations before you. Yes, the circumstances are different, but the circumstances are always different. When the Spartans went to war, they used spears, and it took them weeks to travel the distance we would in seconds in a jet. When the first Americans fought Britain, they had to hide in the brush and utilize guerrilla warfare against a much better-funded military. World War II? Humans were asked to stop the greatest atrocities the world had ever seen."

He put his right index finger on the table and looked at all three of them.

"The world *always* asks the young to do it. It's the young who carry the mantle for nations and civilization alike. I'm here to tell you that there's nothing special about what's being asked of you. History needs the young to protect the old and decrepit like me, and now it's your turn to raise the flag of war." He removed his finger from the table and leaned back in his chair. "I'm also here to tell you that you can do it. That while the request isn't special, you three are. I'm not here to give you a pep talk, because you don't need it. I know you're coming back, and I know you'll do whatever is necessary to serve humanity. So don't get scared, because millions of others have been called before you, and many of them died face-down in the mud. You won't. You're going to be victorious."

He stood and pushed his chair under the table.

"That was all I wanted to tell you. You've joined a long

line of heroes, and now it's time to win the war. It has been a pleasure serving with all of you, including you, Frank." He nodded at the leprechaun. "My part might have been small, but to know you four has been a privilege. I'll see you when you return."

He walked around the far end of the table and slapped Frank lightly on the shoulder. "Thanks for the beer." Dr. Byron left the room without another word.

Jack turned his chair to stare at the closed door. "That man sure knows how to make an exit."

CHAPTER SEVENTEEN

The rules were simple. Cross over, follow Frank, find Prometheus, get powers. They had two days to do it, although Frank had asked for more time. Apparently, the engineers had bigger problems the longer they were there, which wasn't making anyone feel great.

Frank had given the group the scoop on what had happened when he went over, telling them about it in detail. No one was exactly sure where they would arrive. Could be that spot, could be somewhere different. Could be they didn't arrive.

They went to the same room Frank had been in last time, said their good-byes to Lance and Remington, stared at a black ball, and then...

Frank put his hand to his head. "Oh, me heavens. Could our luck get any fucking worse?"

Claire looked around her, almost unable to believe that it had worked. They were standing on a mountain—just as Frank had done last time. The room had disappeared, and the black ball no longer existed. Claire ignored Frank and quickly turned, searching for her friends.

"Don't worry," Jack whispered. "We're here."

He and Marissa were looking around in awe. The mountain rose so high it got lost in the clouds, and they were halfway up it. They stood on a narrow pathway, and if they veered a foot or so too far to the wrong side, they'd quickly find themselves at the bottom. Claire recognized that she couldn't stand here gaping for long. They only had forty-eight hours.

She whipped back to Frank. "This the same place you came in?"

Frank turned with his eyebrows raised. "Lass, are ye mad? Do ye not know where ye are?"

"Sorry, Frank. Haven't been on this particular mountain before. Where the heck are we?" There wasn't time to banter now. They needed to get off this mountain and find Poseidon, like, *yesterday*.

Frank didn't say anything, just sat down in the middle of the pathway. "It's over, lass. We might as well try to make ourselves comfortable for the next few days because we are not getting to Poseidon. Not from here."

Jack and Marissa both turned, and all three stared at the leprechaun.

"Frank, what are you talking about? Where are we?" Claire asked.

Frank pointed at the mountain on his left. "This right here is a dragon roost. That's all fine and dandy because dragons won't come looking for us just because we're here. They only get rambunctious when you get into the roost. The *problem*, me dear humans, is that this dragon roost is a week's travel on horseback from the nearest ocean. There are no dwarves around and no other civilizations because when a dragon gets hungry, it goes looking for food. The smart creatures stay as far away from a dragon's roost as possible."

Jack crossed his arms over his chest. "Are you kidding, Frank? After all this, you're saying it's too far away to travel to?"

Frank nodded. "Yes, lad, that's what I'm telling ye. Our best bet is to wait right here or head down the mountain and find whatever shelter we can for the next two days and hope those dragons don't get hungry."

Marissa was obviously thinking about the idea of hunkering down. "If we wait two days, I mean, it's quite possible Hades and Ares will wreck another city. They might expand their little empire."

Frank shrugged and draped his arms over his knees. "If ye have another idea, I'm open to listening. All I'm telling ye is there's no way we'll make it on foot."

Claire took a step toward the ledge and then looked up at the mountain. "Then we're not going on foot. Where are those dragons, Frank?"

The leprechaun gave a high laugh. "The lass is a dragon-tamer now? Yer going to march up there and demand they fly ye to Poseidon? Fly ye to the ocean? Maybe ye don't know this, lass, but dragons aren't fond of water."

Claire didn't so much as glance at him. "Where are they? Up there? Or do they roost in the middle of the mountain?"

Frank looked exasperatedly at Marissa. "Ye have to talk some sense into her. She's going to get herself killed. Not me, because I won't be going with the crazy woman under any circumstances."

"Claire—" Marissa started.

Claire whirled to face the three of them. "You three stay here. I'm not asking you to go. But I will *not* wait two days, only to go back to the FBI and beg them to send us again when we have no idea where we'll end up *that* time. Maybe we'll end up *inside* the dragon roost next. No. We're here, and I'm completing this mission." She turned to Frank. "Now tell me where the dragons roost."

Frank slowly picked himself up off the ground, then waddled over and stood in front of Claire, looking up at her. "I'm pleading with you, lass. This is folly. Dragons aren't like ye and me. They are little more than beasts. There's no reasoning with them, no asking favors. They want gold and food, and I don't have any more gold. If ye go up there, ye won't return."

Claire nodded. "Up, then. Good. Be ready to jump on the beast when you see me flying by with it. There won't be time to waste. I'm serious about you staying here. If I don't make it, you'll need to be able to tell the FBI what happened."

Frank pointed a finger at her. "We'll tell them ye were a damned fool. Do *not* do this, Claire."

Claire dipped down and quickly kissed the leprechaun's cheek. "Love you, Frank. See you in a few."

She started walking up the mountain. Three minutes later, she turned around and saw them following her, forty or so feet behind. She shook her head. They weren't listening to her, but she knew it would be fruitless to argue. They went where she went, and nothing she told them would change that. Instead, she resumed her march.

Claire didn't have any clue what she would do when she came face to face with a dragon or a bunch of dragons for that matter. She only knew what she'd told them: that there wasn't time to wait. She'd have to figure it out when she got there, but she definitely would be getting onto Dr. Byron for not mentioning dragons in any of his lectures.

Maybe an hour passed before she saw the lair, and she stopped walking and stared. She wasn't near the top of the mountain, but this couldn't be anything else. A hole easily forty feet high and forty feet wide pierced the side of the mountain. She couldn't see inside yet, but she doubted snakes had made this burrow. Her group's footfalls grew louder as they approached.

Frank stopped next to her. "Lass, these creatures are not for men to fight, nor any other species. They are a dangerous lot, and regardless of what ye think ye can do in there, ye can't. We best head down now before they think we're after their gold."

Marissa and Jack remained silent. That was their consent; they would do whatever Claire thought necessary.

She didn't listen to Frank since she was thinking ahead. What in the world could she do to a dragon? Nothing she had learned at school would help her, yet, standing outside this massive lair, she felt...

Like I belong here, she thought. Without looking at Frank, she said, "I'm going in. You have to stay here—all of you, just in case I don't make it back. I know you want to come in, but you can't. If something happens, the world is going to need you."

Marissa walked around the group and stood in front of Claire so that she couldn't avoid looking at her. "Do you have to do this? Isn't there some other way? Like Frank's?"

Claire understood that everyone here thought she was being rash, and perhaps she was, yet she was also right. There wasn't time to waste, and she thought she could do this. Against all odds, she thought she could. "No, there isn't any other way. Not for me. If I can't go inside and get one of the dragons, how am I going to defeat Ares or Zeus?" She shook her head. "No. I'm going in. I'll see you all in a few minutes."

Claire could tell Marissa wanted to hug her, but to do that would be like saying goodbye. Jack stepped up and put his hand on her shoulder. "See you in a few minutes. We will be waiting."

Claire nodded. Frank said nothing else. He was either angry or scared, but he remained quiet. Claire went forward, leaving her friends behind, and into the dragons' lair.

Claire was a hundred feet into the cavern when it hit her. *It isn't pitch-black.*

It should have been because she couldn't see the sun from here, but torches lined the wall. Every ten feet or so, on opposite sides of the wall, another one burned. Claire didn't understand what it meant, because if dragons were like Frank said, they were beasts who couldn't figure out even such crude tools.

Her mother's voice suddenly popped into her mind. *This world isn't for you.*

She shoved it away just as quickly as it had come. There wasn't time for doubt right now. Torches or not, she was finding a dragon and getting the hell out of here. Claire continued onward.

The tunnel wound deep into the mountain, and when it split off, she paused for only a second, then chose her path and kept going. She'd been in dark tunnels before, back when it was vampires she chased and not dragons.

Perhaps she'd been walking tunnels an hour, or maybe two, when she finally heard the creature. She didn't know how far away it was, only that it sniffed the air. Claire froze immediately, goosebumps rising on her arms. The sound was like what Claire imagined a giant would sound like, the noise rushing through the air as if it were a hundred feet tall.

Did ye think it was tiny, lass? Frank asked inside her mind. Apparently, now that she was alone in a dark cavern, all the voices wanted to come out and play.

The beast sniffed again, and this time when it breathed out, it sounded angry. Everything inside Claire was telling her to run. For a moment, she considered it, but her feet didn't move. The creature obviously knew she was here. The time to run had been earlier.

Claire went forward again, the torches leading her through the winding tunnels—until she heard the dragon's first footfall. The noise was ten times louder than its breathing. Claire's eyes widened as the second foot stomped down. It was coming for her, and perhaps more of them if this one could communicate with the others.

Claire stood in the middle of the tunnel, not moving forward anymore but still not leaving. The steps moved in a lazy rhythm as if the stomper knew it didn't have to rush anywhere. It had nothing to fear, and would eventually get to the place it was headed. The footsteps grew louder by the moment, then Claire saw its snout turn the corner.

It was red, with black holes for nostrils and pointed teeth like mountain peaks in its mouth. All the breath in Claire left her, and she felt like she might faint. It was only curiosity that kept her standing. What did the rest of this wondrous creature look like?

Its head came into view, the snout leading up to white eyes with red irises. When it saw her, its eyes flicked her way, and then it...stopped. The beast blinked, not like a mammal, but like an amphibian. After a moment, it slowly took another step forward, then another, until its entire body was in view. Its feet were the size of a dinosaur's, with jagged claws on the toes. Its thighs were tree trunks. Its wings were not in their full glory since they were pulled back.

Everything had those same red scales.

The dragon raised its snout and sniffed again, then lowered it and snorted like a bull might before rushing a matador.

Don't show fear, Claire thought. She wanted to raise her hands in a peace-type gesture, but she kept them at her sides. Her calves were shaking as adrenaline pumped through her body, but she forced them to remain steady. "My name is Claire." It was the first time she'd spoken in these tunnels and her voice echoed off the walls, sounding much louder than she'd intended.

The dragon's eyes narrowed so that Claire could only see the red irises and the black pupils. It lowered its head a bit more and opened its mouth. The bottom row of teeth glowed white in the firelight. The breath rushed from its mouth, and Claire felt a gust of warm air that blew her hair back. Warm wasn't the right word, though. This was *hot*.

All it has to do, Claire thought, *is breathe fire and I'm a goner. It'd fill this entire tunnel with flames.*

Claire tilted her head up. "I need your help."

Again the dragon breathed from its mouth, and this time Claire thought she saw the faintest flicker of fire snake through its teeth before disappearing. The temperature in the tunnel had gone up twenty degrees in seconds.

Claire didn't know what to say now. Did this beast understand English? That was a question she should have asked long ago. There was no running from what lay in this beast's belly. "If you don't help me, my world is going to be destroyed. Billions of creatures just like me. Humans."

The dragon's eyes were little more than slits now. It took one step forward, its head dipping, obviously preparing to set fire to the entire place.

Claire looked at the torch on the wall to her left and shook her head in disbelief. "I know you're not a beast. Not really. No beast creates lights like these, at such perfect intervals. I don't know if you understand my language, but..." Claire turned back to the dragon. "You know I mean you no harm. And I imagine you know I need your help."

The dragon sat straight up, its eyes widening as it reached its full height. It turned its head toward the wall, obviously looking at the torch.

Does it understand? Claire wondered, hope rising in her.

"You created those, didn't you? You keep them alight, and you replace them when there is nothing left to burn. You light this place up, and..."

Now Claire's eyes narrowed. It didn't make sense. Why would the dragon keep these torches lit? Certainly not for its own benefit, since it could simply breathe flames if it needed to see.

Claire's face relaxed, and she smiled. "Oh, my goodness. You've been wanting company. Frank's an idiot. Those torches are to help people find you, aren't they? You're... Are you lonely?"

The dragon took a step back, its eyes narrowing and its teeth flashing again.

Claire put her hands up, her palms facing the dragon. It was her first sign of vulnerability, but she didn't feel nervous about it. This dragon didn't mean her harm, it just didn't want to come off as...weak? "Hey, it's okay. Lonely or not, I'm right, aren't I? You've been wanting some company?"

The dragon's lips lowered over its teeth, the anger disappearing. Claire took a step forward with her palms still raised. The dragon didn't back up, but it did appear nervous.

"You're the only one on this mountain, aren't you?" Claire asked. "There aren't any other dragons, not here, but everyone is so frightened of your kind, they don't know it." Claire's mind was racing, thinking through everything that came with her words. "If they did know, maybe they would come and try to kill you. You're in a tough position. You can't welcome people up here because you're the only one, but you also... You don't want to be alone."

In a very childlike fashion, the dragon dropped its head. "They're all gone."

Claire couldn't help it. She was so shocked she took two steps backward. The dragon had *talked*. The air around her had heated up as it did, but words instead of flames had exited its mouth. The voice was rough, sounding like the scales on its body also made up its vocal cords.

The dragon kept staring at the floor. "I don't know where they went, but my family is gone. I thought they would come back, but they didn't."

Claire moved her mouth to try to form words, but she couldn't think of anything to say. It was strange enough a dragon was standing in front of her, but it was also *speaking?*

The dragon's head slowly lifted, its eyes narrowing again. "Is this a trick? Are you going to return to your land and tell the villagers there's only me up here? Is that why you've come?"

Wide-eyed, Claire shook her head and finally found a word. "No."

The dragon stepped closer. Its footfall sounded like worlds colliding. "Then why are you here? Speak."

"I..." Claire gave an exasperated laugh, dropping her hands and her eyes to the floor. This was so big, she couldn't think of where to begin. "I need your help, and I don't have time to explain why. My friends are outside waiting for me. They probably think I'm dead, but all four of us need your help. I'm rambling now." She tilted her head up. "I need you to take my friends and me to see Poseidon. Do you know who that is?"

The dragon snorted. "You think because I live in a cave that I don't know the world?"

It obviously had insecurity issues, but that made sense, given its family had deserted it. Claire needed to treat this creature kindly. "Not at all. I just didn't want to assume. Can you take us there? Do you know where he is? He's going to introduce us to Prometheus."

The dragon glanced past her, its eyes the size of watermelons. "I've seen Poseidon, and I know Prometheus. I could just take you to him. Dragons see even more than griffins. There isn't anything in this world that can hide from us, except for my family. They're the only thing I haven't been able to find—" The creature stopped speaking, then its eyes widened and its nostrils flared. It breathed in heavily, much like it had done when Claire first entered. "There are others here."

Claire didn't doubt the beast for a second. "Those are my friends. They're idiots because I told them to wait outside, but they love me, so they're coming to look for me. Please don't hurt them. They mean you no harm."

The dragon wasn't looking at her, but past, and it was sniffing the air.

"I'm going to yell for them, okay? I'm going to let them know that no one is in any danger."

The dragon said nothing. Its teeth were bared. It might be lonely, but it was also frightened of strangers. Being the last of your family in a world that feared you wasn't a safe predicament.

Claire slowly turned her head over her shoulder. "Frank! Jack! Marissa! I'm okay! I need you to stay where you are for right now! Do *not* come in any closer!"

She turned back to the dragon. "Can you tell if they've stopped?"

The creature still glared beyond Claire, but said, "I believe so."

"See, they're not going to hurt you. Not that any of us could even if we wanted to. We're just three humans and a leprechaun. You know what humans are?"

The dragon's eyes fell on her once again. "You look like an elf, but your ears are a bit less pointy and you dress differently."

Claire smiled. "That's probably true, although I haven't seen an elf in person. Look, I don't have a ton of time right now. To be honest, I have two days, and then I'm going to be yanked away from this place and sent back to my world." She took a step forward. "Will you help us?"

"I don't understand what you're asking of me," the dragon responded. "Just to take you to Prometheus?"

Claire nodded. "That's right. Nothing else." Something occurred to Claire just then. "When did your family disappear?" She didn't know if the dragon had a sense of time, but it could speak English, so perhaps.

"Two years ago," it answered quietly.

An alarm sounded in Claire's head. *That was around the first time of the first sighting*, she thought. *Could it have to do with what's going on here?* "Why weren't you with them?"

The dragon sat back on its haunches, looking mournful. "I'm the youngest of our pack. Someone had to stay and watch over the mountain. They were supposed to be gone a week. They never returned."

Another realization came to Claire. This dragon might be huge in stature, but it was only an adolescent. Maybe younger than that. If its family had left, it didn't have the knowledge of how to search for them. *Why would they leave the youngest?* she wondered but didn't ask. "Do you know where they went?"

"The Sky God asked to see them. He wanted a meeting between all the different dragon tribes, or at least that's what I understood."

The Sky God, Claire thought. *That can only be Zeus. Two years ago? That was too much of a coincidence. But why would Zeus want to sideline dragons? They lived in the mountains and seemed to be mostly independent creatures.*

There wasn't time for questions. They needed to get to Prometheus, but if Claire was right about this, maybe she could help him find the lost dragons. Or at least find out what happened to them. "Do you have a name?" she asked.

"Falkor," it whispered.

"And forgive me, Falkor. Are you male or female?" Claire asked.

The dragon's eyes widened, and it gave her a look of genuine surprise. "That's insulting. I'm a boy."

Claire tried to hide her grin. "I didn't mean to insult you. It's just...well, I didn't want to take a look for myself. Now listen, Falkor. There is a lot going on here, and I don't understand it all myself, but if you help us, I might be able to find out what happened to your family and any other dragons who were at that summit. I don't know if you can hear me when we fly, but if you can, I'll tell you everything on the way. Will you take us?"

The dragon looked back down the tunnel, probably considering his life here. Two years of loneliness. Two years of waiting for a family to show that never did. When he turned his massive head back to Claire, he nodded. "I'll take you four. That leprechaun, is he a jerk? I've heard they're not to be trusted."

Claire smiled widely and clapped. "That, sir, is probably the truth. This one's name is Frank, and he is a definite jerk, but you can trust him. You ready to meet them?"

"You give me your word you'll try to help me find them? My family?"

"I promise, Falkor. If you help me, I will do my very best to help you."

The dragon started moving forward, and Claire jumped back against the wall so as not to be smashed. "Let's go meet these elf-like creatures and the leprechaun. For his sake, I hope he's as friendly as you."

Claire had to jog to keep up with the beast. His strides were just too long, but as she watched from behind, she realized how majestic he was. It was like watching a dinosaur in real life, a talking one. She still didn't understand that part yet, but she hoped to find out on their flight.

Her group hadn't made it deep into the tunnels yet. They'd only just passed the first bend when they first saw Falkor. Jack screamed, and the dragon stopped walking.

Marissa shouted, "Claire!" None of them could see her behind the massive winged serpent.

Claire ran beneath the dragon's belly and between his legs, stopping just in front of him. Frank's hands were fists, and despite Jack's scream, he'd stepped in front of Marissa. "Guys, guys! It's okay. He's going to help us."

"Move, lass," Frank commanded. "Get out of the way, and then run as if your life depended on it. I'll try to hold the beast back."

Claire felt hot breath exit from Falkor's mouth, and she looked up at him. "No. Please. He just wants to protect me. Give me a minute here before you roast them."

Falkor dipped his head to look at her, then gave the slightest of nods. Claire turned back to her friends. "Frank, listen to me very carefully. This dragon's name is Falkor. He's a boy, and he's young. I don't know the equivalent for humans or leprechauns, but he's *young*. There are no other dragons in this whole mountain, Frank. He's the last one. I don't have time to explain right now, but he's going to help us get to where we're going. Also, I think the disappearance of his family might be connected to everything that's happening."

She took a step forward and focused on Jack and Marissa. "It's okay, you two. Look at me, I haven't been harmed. What we're going to do, in a *very* friendly and orderly fashion, is climb on Falkor's back, and he's going to take us to see Prometheus." She looked at all three. "Does everyone understand that?"

Frank was still staring at the beast as he spoke. "Just how did you come to understand all that information, lass? They leave a written record back there about the family history?"

The dragon's rough, loud voice filled the tunnel. "I told her, you nitwit."

Frank's hands fell open, as did his mouth. "Zeus help me, it talks."

Jack began stuttering. "Whu-whu-what did it just say?"

Claire smiled. "Falkor here can talk, and very well. I don't know if he's speaking English or we're speaking whatever language dragons speak, but somehow it works. Now, can we save the catching up for when we're in the air?"

Marissa was the only one who didn't look shocked. She was staring at the dragon without fear, only wonder. "Folklore from the west says dragons don't talk, but in the east, many myths say dragons are the ones who taught humans to speak." She walked forward, appearing unafraid. She moved past Claire to the dragon's massive foot and placed a gentle hand on his leg. "It would make sense that they can talk, depending on who you asked in the world." She looked up at the giant. "My name is Marissa. Those two assholes over there are Frank and Jack. Frank's the green one. I'd love to go for a ride if you don't mind taking me."

The dragon dipped his head so that his snout was only a few inches from Marissa. His head was nearly the size of her entire body. "You seem nice. I imagine you don't want me to eat your friends either?"

Marissa smiled and shook her head. "Nope. It's not that I like them all that much, just that we're going to need them in the future, I think."

Claire couldn't tell if the dragon was smiling, but it looked like it. His teeth were bared, but there was no menace in it. "Come on, then. Let's go see Prometheus."

CHAPTER EIGHTEEN

Riding the dragon was a tricky endeavor, at least at first. Falkor had never been ridden, so a lot of things one would imagine were necessary weren't around, including saddles and such. That fed Frank's fury at having to trust the dragon, and Claire did her best to settle him down as they worked through the solutions. Falkor led them back to his lair to let them search through what he possessed to find something that might help them remain on his back when the wind buffeted them.

Another two hours had passed by the time they'd rigged up something that *might* keep them on the dragon's back. It was little more than rope and cloth the family had collected over the years, which Falkor had added to during his time alone. Essentially, they were going to tie themselves to the dragon's back, connecting each foot to the other by stretching a rope beneath Falkor's stomach.

"In all me life," Frank mumbled, "I've never seen anything this dumb. I would rather stare Medusa in the face than do this."

Claire didn't comment on his gripes. "Look, we were supposed to meet Poseidon, right, but Falkor says he can take us directly to Prometheus. Can we just do that?"

Frank was staring at the ropes draping off the dragon's back, shaking his head in disgust. "Lass, how am I supposed to know? Ye haven't listened to me since we got over here, so I'm not sure why ye would start now? The plan was for us to get to the ocean, and then Poseidon would take us to Prometheus. Him being a relative and all, he thought he could get the god to see us, plus, he's powerful in his own right. There'd be some danger, but having a god on your side usually aids that some." Frank yelled to Falkor, "Ye big beast, do ye want to take us to the ocean?"

Jack and Marissa were still outfitting his back. Falkor glared at Frank and ignored the question.

"I thought not," Frank said to Claire. "So, it doesn't look like we have much choice but to do it your way. I don't know if Prometheus is going to accept us or attack us, but I guess we're going to find out. A whole plan thrown away because of yer stubbornness." Frank stormed off, and Claire let him go. She knew she was making the right decision. The other way might be safer, but it would take too long. Right now, she'd accept risk to save time—plus, it had worked out with Falkor here.

"We're just about ready!" Jack called from across the cavern. "If any of you fall off, blame it on Marissa. It's certainly not my fault."

Claire rolled her eyes, then yelled to Frank. "Quit sulking! Time to go."

Claire sat closest to Falkor's neck, and when she bent down to his scales, the wind passed right over her. She was forced to hug him, but his scales also served as handles that helped her keep her balance. All of them had managed to lodge their feet beneath them, with Falkor assuring them he didn't feel a thing.

His booming, jagged voice told them, "It's like armor. Direct hits with arrows just bounce off."

And now Claire was soaring through the air in a way she had never imagined. There was a cocoon of silence wrapped around her, the aerodynamics of the dragon keeping the wind from attacking her or those behind her. No one said a word, though, not even Frank. They were all too mesmerized to consider speaking. They flew just beneath the clouds, with Falkor taking them up into them every once in a while.

"Why do ye keep doing that?" Frank yelled from the back.

Falkor must have been able to hear him perfectly because he tilted his head slightly to the left and said, "I see more than you do, little one. When I move up, there is danger. When I move back down, it's for your viewing benefit."

Frank grumbled something, but Claire couldn't hear a word of it. She didn't care either. The sights below were just too amazing. Rivers and trees, huts and homes...she even saw a pack of deer running through an open field. It was like flying on an airplane, only on the outside and without the fear of death.

Well, almost without the fear of death.

A little while later, the dragon turned his head again. "We have time. Will you explain why you're all here?"

Claire had told the story so many times that she was growing tired of it, yet she knew Falkor deserved it, having put his adolescent trust in her. She dove into the tale, leaving nothing out and not caring how much time passed. She wanted him to know it all, just as she had told her parents. She even told him about the connection between his family and the timing of the first Mythers crossing over.

"The part I don't get," she continued, "is why Zeus would want to get rid of the dragons before he started all this."

Falkor twisted his head again. "You really think he might have had something to do with my family disappearing?"

"I think it's a strong possibility," she answered. "Everything I know about that god is bad. I just don't know why."

"And unfortunately for Zeus, I don't care why." The dragon turned back forward and was silent as they flew.

The sun was descending when Falkor finally started circling an area. He stayed inside some cloud cover, but Claire could see beneath. The dragon twisted his snout. "This is where he is."

Frank spoke from behind. "This makes no sense. The dragon is out of his gourd."

Claire didn't understand what she was looking at either. They were circling over a river, one that had heavy forests on either side. Claire couldn't see any animals, let alone Prometheus. "Where is he, Falkor?"

The dragon was slowly making his way to the ground,

losing altitude with each circle. "Prometheus lives under the ground. He fears that if he were to live above, where the creatures of the air might report him back to Zeus, he'd end up having another bird peck at him for all eternity. So, he lives beneath that river."

Jack asked the next question. "Then how have you seen him? You never mentioned an ability to see through water?"

The dragon increased his angle, causing everyone to grab on tighter. Claire thought it might have been his way of getting back at Jack's question. He straightened after a few moments. "The god comes up every now and then, and I've spent a long time looking for my family. I've seen him a few times."

"How do you know it's him?" Claire asked.

The dragon didn't look back this time, only said, "You'll see."

They continued dropping until finally they landed on the northern bank of the river. The trees were about thirty feet from them and the entire forest was silent, the animals perhaps understanding a dragon was here. Falkor seemed not to notice. The group unhooked their feet and hopped off. Claire stretched as she watched the river rush in front of her. Falkor nodded toward it. "Prometheus is under the river."

Frank waddled up to the edge. "This dragon might talk, but he doesn't have more than five brain cells inside that head of his. How in the world is he underneath the river? Poseidon didn't mention anything about a damned river."

Falkor flapped his large wings once, causing wind to tousle Claire's hair, then folded them against his body. "I don't know what Poseidon knows. Perhaps he had another way inside. Perhaps there are tunnels beneath this river that lead to the ocean, and he could have gotten you in that way. All I know is that I can show you the entrance here."

Claire looked up at the dragon. "You're not going in with us?"

The dragon turned so that his snout pointed at the ground at her feet. "I can't fit inside. I can stand guard here, and if you flee, I can make sure anything coming after you won't make it away from the river. Down there, though, it's up to you. I've brought you here, Claire. You promise you will do your part and try to figure out what happened to my family?"

Claire walked over and touched Falkor's scaled leg, her hand tiny against his hugeness. "I promise. Thank you for bringing us here. When we come back out, I promise I'll have information about your family. More than I do now, at least."

Frank's back still faced the group. "Just how ye going to get us in?"

The dragon looked up, his voice rough. "Watch out, wee one."

Frank heard something in the creature's voice he didn't like. He looked over his shoulder and saw the dragon sucking in a huge breath of air. Falkor's stomach stretched out, and he leaned backward. Frank knew what was coming and wasted no time; he teleported immediately, landing right next to Claire.

Falkor leaned forward. His body stretched far beyond his legs, his heavy tail balancing him. He opened his mouth, and Claire felt the heat before she saw the fire. Flames blazed from his mouth in a straight line, and in seconds it lit the river. The water sizzled and tried to fight the fire, but it kept coming from Falkor's mouth in a never-ending torrent of flames. It stretched across the entire river, and as it did, the water downstream flowed away. Vast plumes of steam rose into the air, but the dragon didn't tire.

Sure enough, he had been right. As the water was halted by his fire, a massive hole directly beneath the river was revealed. "How is that even possible?" Claire wondered aloud. It appeared that the water had been rushing right over it, yet the cavern was far too large for it not to simply flow into it.

"No time, lass," Frank snapped. "We have to get in there before the dragon's fire runs out. It's not unlimited. Let's just hope whatever sorcery keeps the water out continues to do so."

Frank rushed toward it, with Jack right behind him. Marissa and Claire were still staring at the thing in wonder. Claire finally shook her head. "Let's go."

They ran forward. The guys had already climbed down the banks, and we're now running across its muddy bottom. The cavern had a staircase that wound around its side in a circular fashion. Frank was the first one to make it, and he skipped down the first twenty steps or so. Jack was right behind him.

The flames were burning about forty feet up the river on Claire's right. The heat made her brow and hair heavy with sweat. She took a quick glance over her shoulder, and what she saw terrified her. The dragon was running out of fire. Not completely, but the flames exiting his mouth weren't as solid, and they were starting to sputter.

If the flames gave out, this river would wash over her and Marissa, killing them both. "*Hurry!*" she shouted and picked up her pace. The mud was slippery beneath her feet. Every couple of steps, she found herself nearly face-planting as her feet slid out from under her. She lost sight of Marissa and focused on getting to the cavern before Falkor gave out.

Five feet.

Two.

She was in, quickly making it down the first few steps. Frank and Jack were in front of her, but where was Marissa?

No, she thought frantically and rushed back up the steps. When she reached the top, Marissa was on her knees thirty feet away, struggling to get back up. *She's sprained something.* Claire didn't have time to waste since the fire from Falkor's mouth was almost gone. The wall of fire to the left was dying, and strands of the river were making their way through.

Claire ran as fast as she could. Marissa was hobbling. Her right leg looked like it might give out on her. She wasn't going to make it without Claire, and neither might get to the cavern.

Claire reached her friend, gasping for breath.

"No," Marissa said. "*No!* What the hell are you doing? Why did you come out here?"

"Because we're a team." Claire didn't quit moving as she spoke. There was no way the two of them would make it with both trying to run. She simply grabbed Marissa and threw her over her shoulder.

Marissa screamed at her to leave her, but Claire

hardly heard it. She simply let her feet pound the muddy ground beneath her and did the best she could to keep from slipping. From her peripheral vision, she saw that the fire was nearly gone. Streams of water ran in front of and behind her. They were growing thicker by the second.

And then she heard the wall of fire give way all at once. The sound of the water breaking through was like thunder. Without slowing, she looked to her right and saw death coming.

"*DROP ME!*" Marissa screamed.

Claire held her tighter, put her head down, and *ran*.

Five feet.

The sound of flooding water felt like it might break her eardrums.

Three feet.

She could feel the spray on her cheek.

Claire hit the first step of the circular staircase and fell. Her ass hit the step and then slid down to two more. The water *whooshed* overhead, but it didn't fall into the pit. The sound was deafening, as if the water was beating against some thin, invisible layer above. Claire helped Marissa off her, and both looked down at Frank and Jack. The two stared back up, wide-eyed and pale of face.

Claire slowly regained her feet and then pointed behind the two guys. "*LET'S GO!*" she shouted to be heard above the river's roar. Marissa draped her arm around Claire's shoulders and the crew started down.

The farther they went, the darker it grew until they could hardly see anything. The sound above had faded, and eventually, Frank came to a stop. "I can't see anything, and I know me eyes are better than ye humans'. How deep do ye think this goes?"

Claire was almost blind at this point. "I've got no idea, but we don't have any other choice right now. We got through something similar back in the funhouse. Jack, can you help Marissa, and I'll take the lead?"

Claire couldn't see him, but she heard the humor in his voice. "I've been carrying her since I first met her. No reason I shouldn't carry her now too." Claire felt him grab Marissa's other arm, releasing her of her duty. She carefully moved past Frank and went down another step. Just as she was about to take one more, a light appeared to her left. It was purple and appeared to be floating. Everyone looked at once.

The light started as a very small ball but grew quickly, doubling in size in five seconds. Claire could finally see where she was and realized they'd reached the bottom. The next step would have put her on flat rock. She glanced up and was mesmerized by how far they had come down. She didn't want to consider what it would be like to bring Marissa back up then. She turned back to the light. "What is it, Frank?"

"Ye think I know, lass? I don't hang around in these parts." He was a few feet above Claire, and he hopped to the ground. He walked over to the ball of light and stared up at it. "I think it's some kind of alerting device because it didn't turn on until we were at the bottom. If you ask me, this ain't good."

Claire stepped up next to Frank, although she looked over her shoulder at Jack and Marissa. "Marissa, you have any idea what this is?"

"No," she said, sounding like she was in a lot of pain. "No idea. Prometheus is known as a trickster, though, so I wouldn't trust anything we see down here. Especially not if he's hiding from Zeus."

Claire looked around the circular walls. She found what she wanted pretty fast. She pointed at the arch. "Looks like we can only go back up or through there. Let's keep going. Jack, do you need help with Marissa, or are you good?"

"I've never needed help before, so we shouldn't start now," he quipped. "I'm good. Frank, what was the plan if we had met Poseidon? Like, did you go into depth about what to expect?"

Frank was still staring at the purple light. He shook his head. "Main thing was, if we could convince Prometheus to fight against Zeus, he'd give Claire powers. The god said it would be a treacherous journey, and we might not make it. That's it."

Claire had reached the arch, and she turned around. "You're not much of a researcher, are you?"

Frank finally pulled himself away from the light. "Ye tell me how ye do when ye've nearly drowned and a god tells ye to just listen. Come on. I'm tired of dealing with these Greeks. I want to get this over with." He passed Claire and entered the tunnel. Claire waited until Jack and Marissa had gone in front of her and brought up the rear.

When she stepped under the arch, the floating purple light followed, keeping a safe distance behind. "We've got company!" Claire called to the front of the line.

Marissa turned back around and looked at the light. "It's an eye. Something is watching us."

That sent a chill down Claire's spine. There wasn't anything she could do about it, though, except go forward.

Claire couldn't imagine hiding in a place like this, certainly not for as long as Prometheus had. It was a dank, cold place filled with endless tunnels, and Frank was grumbling nonstop. The purple light remained a good distance behind them, following like some kind of silent tour guide.

Frank stopped walking and turned around to stare at it. Claire stopped too since she didn't know where they were going. This was a labyrinth that felt like it had no end. Frank walked past Marissa and Jack, then got right below the light. "The damned dragon might have lied to me, and if I see him again, I'm going to kick his ass from one side of the Veil to the next, but I'm down here looking for ye Prometheus, and ye know it. Why don't you just tell me where ye are?"

Claire couldn't be sure, but she thought the light glowed a bit brighter.

"Ye know we are here. Show yourself, trickster!" Frank shouted, raising a fist in the air and shaking it at the light.

When the next voice spoke, it didn't emanate from the light, but from the walls. "This is an odd group I see before me, and above, a dragon stopped my river from flowing for a time. I believe three of you are humans and the other is a leprechaun. It makes me wonder why you have come since I figure it was the pesky dragon who brought you to me."

Frank turned to Claire. "Ye better talk to him since I'm liable to curse him out right now."

"It's a long story," Claire said to the light, unsure if that was what she should be talking to.

The walls spoke again. "Trust me, human, you have nothing but time down here. How long have you been walking? How long will you walk? No one knows, because the tunnels down here go forever and they lead nowhere."

Marissa was still hanging on Jack's shoulder and favoring her right foot. "They might be mirages or tricks. They might not really exist. We could just be walking in place right now."

Claire believed Marissa was probably right. If this god was full of tricks, wouldn't that be a grand one, having them walking around until they collapsed from exhaustion? "We need your help against Zeus. Do you know about the Veil?"

"Ahh," the walls whispered. "That is why you're here and why the dragon is alone above."

Claire shook her head. "I don't understand. You know what's happening?"

The walls chuckled at her in mocking judgment. "It is my business to know what Zeus does, lest he find me and give me to one of his little birds again. I've known for some time he's been trying to cross the Veil, but he must have already done it."

"What did you mean about the dragon being alone?" Claire asked. "What does that have to do with any of it?"

The walls' words were like cold drafts through the tunnels. "Silence, human. You do not come to my home and ask me questions. Why are you here? What kind of help do you desire?"

Claire glanced at Frank, who stared back at her. He shrugged. "Tell him ye want some powers."

Claire put her hands on her hips and regarded the leprechaun. After a moment, she looked back up at the light. "Poseidon told my friend here you might be willing to help us. On my side of the Veil, there is a myth you gave fire to humanity. We need you to give us something now to stop Zeus and his brother."

"Hmmm. I heard Hades went across the Veil on a search to find his ghosts, and I guess he found the place to his liking." When they next spoke, the walls sounded as if they were focusing on Claire now. "So, you wish me to just give you something to help fight a god. Indeed, you ask me to turn on my kin. Is that right?"

Claire didn't say anything. It didn't sound like he wanted an answer but was mocking her. She heard Jack and Marissa walk up next to her. Jack leaned close to her ear and said, "This guy is a jackass, and that's saying something, coming from me."

Claire ignored him and kept looking at the light. "Yes, that's what I'm asking. We were told you and Zeus aren't exactly friendly, and given the place in which you live, that's probably true. Will you help us?"

The walls laughed then, and heartily. "If Zeus crosses the Veil, it seems like a good deal to me. Why would I not like him to abandon this world and leave me in peace?" The voice paused for a moment before continuing. "However, I do get bored down here, and I would enjoy rankling Zeus. What can you offer me if I help?"

All eyes fell on Frank. The leprechaun turned his palms up.

Claire glared at him, anger rising in her. "Did Poseidon tell you about this?"

Frank closed his eyes as if trying to avoid everyone's stares. "He didn't get into the details."

The walls interrupted the spat. "So, you bring me nothing, but you come asking for gifts. As your myth says, I didn't bring fire to mortals out of love for them. I brought it to make Zeus mad."

Claire's hands turned to fists. "*This* will make him mad. Helping *me* will make him mad."

"Yes, yes, perhaps," the walls agreed lazily. "But it would be in my best interest to let Zeus cross over. Let me think about this for a minute." Without waiting for a reply, the ball of purple light extinguished, and the group was left in the dark.

Jack helped Marissa to the wall and supported her gently as she blindly sat down. Straightening back up, he said, "Well, Frank, I think you outdid yourself on this one. There's no way in hell we can find our way out of here. I guess we just wait in the darkness until the FBI pulls us back over?"

Claire could hear Frank shuffling over to the wall as well. He took a seat. "Ye three didn't listen to me. Not once did I say we should trust that dragon and end up in these catacombs. It's Claire who's outdone herself. I won't hear any more of ye putting the blame on me."

Claire slowly backed to the wall and lowered herself to the ground. "Stop it, both of you. Marissa, any idea what's going to happen next?"

Pain filled her voice, but she didn't complain. "I imagine

some kind of test. He doesn't seem like the type to simply give us what we want."

"He's a real dick," Jack mumbled. "At least when I'm a dick, you know it's coming from a good place."

Claire wondered what Falkor was doing. Regardless of what Frank said, she liked the dragon. He'd helped them in their time of need. "Anyone have any idea how much time has passed?" The group was silent, their answer unanimous. No one had a clue.

Minutes passed, turning into hours. Claire laid down and dozed for a bit. When she woke up, it was still pitch-black, but she felt someone sitting very close to her.

"It's me, lass," Frank whispered. "Don't make too much noise. The others are sleeping, and I don't want to wake them up. Frank has a plan, and I need you to listen to it."

Claire pulled herself up so her back was against the wall. "A plan?"

Frank sighed. "Yes. I'm going to save the day again. I won't mention to ye what I did with my gold to get us here, but there's more I can do, and I suppose I will."

Claire elbowed him softly. "Get on with it. What's the plan?"

"Despite the current circumstances, leprechauns are lucky. I honestly think ye are the reason I haven't been lucky lately, but that's neither here nor there. This god, he knows it would be lucky to have a leprechaun. There are more rainbows and pots of gold, and I can get them for him."

Claire turned toward her friend, although she couldn't see him. "What are you trying to say, Frank?"

"What we have to give is me," the leprechaun told her.

"If he gives you three something to combat the bastard, I'll pledge myself to him. Frank will turn into his slave, then ye three will go back and battle those two assholes and the third one who hasn't shown himself yet."

Claire was stunned. What Frank had just offered...it was slavery. He'd have to serve this god forever, going out and searching for gold or whatever else the creature wanted. It took her a second to regain her wits. "Frank, the only thing I have to tell you is *no*. You're not giving yourself to this god or anyone else. We came over here together, and we're going to leave together. Plus, when they pull us back, they'll pull us all back."

Frank lightly tapped her thigh. "I imagine this creature can think of ways to keep me from being pulled over, but I see no alternative, lass. If they do pull me over, that's even better. I won't have to be a slave for long. It's our best shot."

Claire shook her head resolutely. "No chance. Not happening. Get that thought out of your head. I won't even entertain it. Don't mention to the others because it's the dumbest thing you've ever come up with."

"I think he's coming back," Frank responded.

Claire saw what the leprechaun meant. The purple light was slowly coming back to life, illuminating the area around the four. Claire looked at Frank. "Not a word about that nonsense. I mean it." She hopped to her feet. "Jack, Marissa, the god is back."

Jack blinked a few times and slowly sat up. "I was having a good dream. This guy really is an asshole." He looked at Marissa, who was sleeping next to him. "You okay?"

She nodded, although her face was pale. "Yeah. My ankle just hurts like hell."

Jack helped her sit up and then gently pulled up the pants leg. "You think it's broken."

Marissa shook her head. "I don't know, but we don't have time." She pointed at the light. "He's almost here."

Claire understood, as did Marissa, that they'd have to deal with her pain when they got back. Right now, they needed to figure out what this god wanted in exchange for his help. The one thing she wouldn't give him was Frank. Or any of her friends, for that matter.

The walls came back to life. "You're all still here. I'm very glad to see that. I've thought about what I want from you, and I was quickly coming to the conclusion that there isn't anything you can give me. I want Zeus gone more than I want to aggravate him. I don't like living down here, only venturing up when I don't think Zeus or his spies will see me. And then..."

The walls' voice trailed off for a moment, and Claire felt her heart sink. The god had heard Frank. He probably heard everything down here, and that was why he'd returned so quickly. Prometheus had heard what Frank offered.

The walls started speaking again. "Your leader knows what I'm about to ask, don't you?"

Jack and Marissa both looked at Claire. "What's it talking about?"

Claire ignored Jack's question and focused on the god. "No. You can't have him. I don't care what either of you says."

Jack stood and stepped away from the wall. "Have *who*, Claire? Tell us what's going on."

It was Frank who did the talking, though. He stood up and rubbed his right hand through his hair. "I told Claire that I would give myself to Prometheus in exchange for him giving you all powers."

Jack raised his hand to stop Frank from talking. "What the hell do you mean, give yourself to him? That doesn't make any damn sense."

The walls chuckled. "Clearly this one is the dullest of the bunch. In exchange for me giving you what you want to defeat Zeus or whoever else is over there now, the leprechaun will do my bidding."

Marissa very slowly made her way to her feet. "You're going to be his slave? That's what you offered? Did you tell Claire?"

"Yes, lass," Frank whispered. "She told me no, as I had expected, but the trickster was listening."

Marissa looked at the light. "That was the whole point, wasn't it? The trick was letting us sit here until we mentioned something we could give, and then you would decide if you wanted it or not." Her pale face took a look of anger.

The walls said, "If you had figured that out earlier, perhaps you wouldn't be in such a predicament, but then again, you would not be in a position to gain what you so desperately want. So, there is good and bad."

Claire stepped in front of Frank, blocking the light's view of him. "It doesn't matter. You can't have him. There must be something else. There has to be since that's out of the question."

Again, the wall laughed at her—a menacing, pitying laugh. "You do not get to decide what happens and what doesn't in here, despite what you might want. I'm speaking to the leprechaun, not you or your little friends. Frank, is that your wish? To bind yourself to me, and in exchange, I'll give these humans powers that will help them stop the invasion of their world?"

Claire whirled to face Frank. "No. Don't even think about it. Not for anything."

Frank was looking at her, his face solemn and his eyes sympathetic. He took Claire's hand. "There's no other way, lass. Not right now. If we had more time or more to bargain with, I'd agree with ye. But we don't."

Claire shook her head violently. "I don't give a damn, Frank. I'm not leaving you here with that monster."

Frank gave her a sad smile. "Unfortunately, me dear, the world depends on ye doing exactly that."

Hot tears filled Claire's eyes. She wanted to rip her hand away from Frank's. She wanted to throw him against a wall and then use her fists to bring down this entire cavern. She felt the first tear drip out of her eye. Frank went up on his tiptoes, and with his free hand, wiped away the tear.

"Don't cry, lass. It won't be so bad. I imagine this here god will let Frank bowl and drink as much as I'd like." He pulled his hand away from her face. "You know it's the right decision. You know it's the *only* decision. One life isn't worth every human life, even if I don't think too highly of ye creatures."

The tears came in full now. Claire couldn't hold them back. She understood that what she wanted didn't matter here. She had no control over Frank and this god. "I don't care," she cried. "*I don't care*. I won't sacrifice you for the world. I won't sacrifice anyone for it."

Frank shook his head, still holding her hand. "It's not your call to make, lass. It's mine and mine alone. Ye aren't sacrificing anyone. I am."

Jack walked up next to Frank and put his hand on the leprechaun's shoulder. "Are you sure this is what you want to do?"

"It's what I have to do, lad." Frank grinned at Jack. "Plus, I want you to sing songs of my heroism and bravery. I want the world to sing them until the sun burns out. Ye understand?"

Tears welled in Jack's eyes as he nodded. "I understand. Humans will sing about a little green leprechaun until the world goes dark."

Frank clapped Jack on the thigh. "That's the spirit."

Marissa had slowly made her way over to him. She didn't say anything, simply reached down and hugged him. Frank's eyes widened at the shock of such a gesture. He slowly put his arms around Marissa. "Careful now, lass. Don't get me excited."

Marissa pulled back, laughing between tears, and slapped him lightly on the shoulder. "Quit it, Frank."

Jack and Marissa stood on either side of the two. Claire was full-on crying, unable to come to terms with what was happening. She hadn't come here to give up her friend, yet she didn't have a choice in the matter. "Please don't do this, Frank. Please. We'll find another way."

He took both of her hands in his. "There isn't time. Ye have to get back and kick those gods' arses. And hey, it's not like I'm sentencing meself to death. Just giving a little of my luck away for a time."

But Claire knew it wasn't "for a time," it was forever. She pulled her hands away from Frank and turned to the light. "If you do this, I promise that when I'm done over there in my world, I'm coming back here." Claire's hands were fists, rage overtaking her sadness. "There is nothing, absolutely nothing, that will stop me from destroying this place and you. Do you understand me?"

The walls' laughter was nearly deafening. It took long moments for it to subside enough for the god to speak. "Girl, you are no more a threat to me than the ant that walks the ground. Save your threats for someone who cares. Leprechaun, do you agree to this deal? You will bind yourself to me and my will, and I will give these humans powers that might help them beat Zeus and whoever else he sends?"

Behind Claire, Frank whispered, "I agree to it."

Claire's nails bit into her palms, and she ground her teeth until her jaw ached, but there was nothing she could do.

"So be it," the walls said. "Leprechaun, walk toward the light."

Frank stepped around Claire, passing her to reach the purple light. "No," she said. "Please, no."

He looked over his shoulder and grinned. "Don't worry, lass. I am sure ye will find a way to give all those Greek gods hell." He winked. "I'll see ye soon."

As he reached the light, standing just beneath, the purple orb expanded. It was as if the globe reached down and grabbed Frank, then quickly resumed its normal state.

He was gone; where he'd been standing was empty space, a cobblestone walkway where his feet had been.

Claire felt Jack and Marissa step up next to her. She ignored them and spoke to the light. "What did you do with him? Where is he?"

"Girl," the walls responded, "he is safe. I won't hurt my good luck charm. Plus, it is no longer your concern what happens to him."

Claire raised her hand as if to grab the light, but Marissa gently took hold of it. She shook her head and firmly made Claire lower it to her side.

The walls chuckled. "The dumb one, the angry one, and the smart one. I'm sure you can figure out which is which. Now, while I was waiting for you to tell me what I wanted from you, I did a little research on my end. It seems that Zeus endowed some humans with powers, which, to be honest, really pissed me off, given what he did to me over a bit of fire. Knowing that, it gave me time to think about what would best help you. I, of course, am a god of my word. From what I can tell, Zeus gave some our shapeshifting abilities, and others super strength, teleportation, and the ability to create fire. All in all, pretty simple things, but that's because he didn't want anyone challenging his supremacy."

The walls yawned then as if this were all very boring. The tears had quit flowing down Claire's face. Now they were drying, but her anger wanted to erupt like a volcano. *Especially* after that yawn.

"So," the god continued, "knowing what and who you'll be facing, I'm going to imbue you with powers that will give you a fighting chance. Not to kill the gods, mind you, but enough to make sure they don't want to mess with you. Smart one, are you paying attention?"

Marissa, tears drying on her face, tilted her head. "I am."

"I'm going to grant you two sets of powers, both stemming from the power of your mind. You will have telepathy and telekinesis. The power to speak without words and to move objects without moving."

The light very quickly grew bright, so much so that Claire's hands reflexively covered her eyes. As soon as it'd lit up, it dulled again. The walls kept talking without pause. "Do not marvel yet. I want your little group out of here as quickly as possible. Dumb one, you listening?"

Jack's face reflected his rage. "Go fuck yourself."

"Unfortunately," the walls said, "your brain isn't powerful enough to be endowed with what I gave the other. Instead, we must use your body. I'm going to grant you the strength of Hercules and the speed of Hermes. Physically, you will be a match for any creature you come up against, although I hope you do not challenge them to a test of wits."

The light brightened and then dulled.

"Finally, the angry one. The leader. The one who threatens to come back and finish me off for agreeing to terms set by your friend." The god chuckled. "Your power will be your will. Indeed, perhaps it is your strongest asset already. This power cannot be used often, and the toll will be great, but if you can figure it out, you might just defeat your foes. Dare I say, if you figure it out, you might be able to defeat *me* when you come back."

The light glowed bright once more and then returned to its normal color.

Claire felt nothing. "You didn't do anything."

No, he did, Marissa said. *Without a doubt, he did something.*

The voice was in Claire's mind, not her ears, yet there was no doubt it was Marissa.

The light rose higher. "Now," the walls said, "it is time for you to leave. When this light blinks out, you will be back at the top of the stairs that brought you to me. Do not come back down here looking for your friend. Not now, not ever, because it will mean death for you. I wish you luck against my brethren, as long as your luck does not interfere with mine. Goodbye."

Claire couldn't hold it any longer. She screamed with rage, her anger ripping from her mouth at the purple light, the walls, at everything this god embodied. As she screamed, the light died in front of her, fading to blackness.

Then they stood about ten feet from the top of the spiral staircase, the pit next to them. Above them, Claire could see the river rushing across the hole, some form of magic keeping it from drowning them. Her scream caught in her throat, her fingernails still digging into her palms.

Jack was just behind her and put his hand on her shoulder. "There's nothing we can do now. Nothing except go up."

Claire took a deep breath, trying to relax. She let her hands slacken and stared at the dark water rushing over them. Without turning her head to look at her friends, she said, "One way or another, I'm coming back for Frank. I'm going to free him, and this god will get what he deserves for this."

"We know," Marissa said as she tried to take one of the

stairs. Her leg almost gave out, and Jack sprang to catch her. Marissa's eyes widened and she opened her mouth to speak, but no words came out.

Jack grinned. "You saw that, huh?"

"Saw what?" Claire asked without looking at them. She kept her eyes on the river.

Marissa finally found her voice. "That's the thing—I didn't see anything. He was standing above me, and then he was here."

Claire looked over her shoulder. "And you can obviously use telepathy. It looks like whatever he did worked with you too, but there's nothing different about me. Right now, I don't want to believe I traded Frank for nothing, so we need to figure out how to get out of here." An idea struck Claire. "Marissa, can you use your mind to see if Falkor is still there?"

Marissa's arm was slung over Jack's shoulder. "He is."

"Maybe this will work, then," Claire thought aloud. "Can you contact him and see if he can use his fire against the river once more?"

Bracing herself against Jack, Marissa put one foot on the next stair. "We don't need to. I can open it."

Claire turned all the way around. "You can what?"

"Jack," Marissa said, "help me get closer to the top."

Jack didn't try to walk with her. He simply wrapped one arm around her hips, gently raised her as if she were a pillow, then set her down when they were a few steps from the top. "There you go, Sissy."

Claire watched as Marissa closed her eyes. A few seconds passed, and then... The dark river above was growing lighter, meaning the water flow was lessening. As the moments passed, the river went from nearly black to not there. Marissa's face strained with concentration. "We have to hurry. It's powerful."

"Not to worry," Jack responded. "Get up here, Claire. We're going across quickly."

Claire climbed the steps until she stood next to her friends. "Don't get handsy with me, Jack, and for the love of goodness, don't drop me."

Jack smirked as he side-eyed her. "Please. You're not my type." He wrapped his arm around Claire's waist, just as he had Marissa's. Claire could see the sky now that the river was gone. Jack lifted her, and she realized what he'd been gifted with. There was no effort, no strain. He simply picked her up and...*took off.*

She barely saw the world around her. It was all a blur, the river practically nonexistent in her vision. He came to a gentle stop once they reached the far bank, setting them both down. "There."

Marissa sighed, and Claire heard the *whoosh* of water rushing through the riverbed. She turned to watch once more. It wasn't fire that had held back its strength this time, but Marissa's mind.

Falkor took a step toward the group. "You're missing one."

Claire kept her eyes on where the hole had been. "For now. But I'll be back to get him."

Falkor made no further comment, perhaps hearing the raw emotion in Claire's voice. "Did you find out about my family?"

Claire brought her eyes to the dragon's. "I found out enough to know that Zeus is behind their disappearance.

Prometheus wouldn't tell me why, but we're not done with him." She took a few steps closer to the beast, keeping their eyes locked. "Do you want to help me? Not defeat the gods attack Earth, but to defeat the one down there? When I put the screws to him, I'm going to get back the one he took. I also think we can get back the ones Zeus took. First, though, we have to go back to Earth and hurt some bad people. When that's over, we're coming back here to hurt the rest of the bad people."

Falkor stared at her for long seconds. His red eyes were contemplative, as if he was trying to see how this all would play out. Claire didn't drop his gaze, and her friends stood silently watching their leader bargain with the dragon.

Falkor nodded slowly, his giant head swinging through the air. "I'll help, as long as you're serious about getting that god to tell me what happened."

"I've never been more serious about anything in my life," Claire responded. "Come to Earth, and when this is finished, we will either reunite with the people we love or make the ones who took them pay."

The dragon lowered his head until it was inches from Claire's nose. "You have a deal."

Jack raised a hand. "One question. How do you think we're going to get this guy to Earth?"

"Leave that to me," Claire answered.

CHAPTER NINETEEN

It happened as the FBI said it would. When the forty-eight hours were up, Claire, Jack, and Marissa were pulled across the Veil and ended up in the same room they'd left from. What came next was a whirlwind of frustration for Claire. Remington and Lance practically rushed to the group with questions. What happened to Frank? Is he alive? Where is he? When did you last see him? Did you get any powers?

On and on the questions went, with Claire knowing she needed to do two things: convince the FBI that they had to pull one more creature over and call her parents.

At first, they didn't want to hear about her needs. They wanted examples of the powers. Marissa and Jack did as they were told, displaying feats of mind and muscle. When the agents looked at Claire, she had no answers to give them. "This is what the god told me. That's it. That's all I know."

Eventually, she managed to get them to hear her.

"There's a dragon over there. We have to bring him over here. He's going to help us."

Of course, that did nothing but lead to more questions. Whose dragon? Is it dangerous? Why must it come? Can it be controlled? In the end, though, the answer was simple.

Remington told her from safely across the table. "We don't have the ability to pull creatures from there unless we put them there. The IT guys and scientists can't figure it out. It doesn't matter what you want with this dragon because we don't have the capability to do it."

Marissa and Jack sat next to her, both of them quiet during this. If Falkor was anyone's, he was Claire's, and she was the only one who could convince the FBI they needed him. "I can get him over."

Remington raised an eyebrow. "Yeah? You can do something our greatest minds haven't been able to?"

"So far, I've done many things none of you could do. So, yes, if you show me how you use that machine, I'll find him and bring him over."

Lance glanced at Claire's hand. It wasn't the first time the agents had noted the bandage, but it was the first time they asked about it. "What's that, Claire? You haven't mentioned the injury to your hand yet."

Claire turned her palm up. She'd ripped off the bottom of her shirt and wrapped it around the wound. The t-shirt was now red with blood, but the cut was no longer bleeding. "That's how I'm going to find Falkor."

Remington leaned on the table. "What did you do, Claire?"

"We know you're able to track us across the Veil using our DNA. I made sure some of my blood was flowing inside Falkor. That means we'll be able to track him and pull him over."

Lance chuckled and shook his head in disbelief. "You sound like a child, Claire. Yes, your DNA is used, but there's a lot more that goes into it, and a lot of DNA needs to be accessible. A few drops of blood? That's not going to cut it. There isn't any way you'll be able to find that dragon."

Claire figured they would say that, and she had planned on ignoring them. "What's the harm in trying? If I can't get him, there's nothing to worry about. If I do get him, we have a dragon on our side to help stop what's happening."

Still leaning forward in his chair, Lance looked at Remington. "What do you think?"

Remington shook his head, his weariness hanging off him like a suit. "I think our bosses will try anything right now, and I think I probably will too. Claire, are you sure this dragon is on our side? If we pull something else over and it attacks us, we're not going to be super-prepared for it."

"First, we're more prepared than you think." Claire pointed at Jack. He grabbed the corner of the desk, and without straining, bent the metal down. Claire looked back at Remington. "Second, I'm sure Falkor is going to help us. The *only* way I can get Frank back is by beating these gods over here and then going back to beat Prometheus. Falkor is going to give me the best chance of doing that."

Remington stood up. "Give us an hour."

The two FBI agents left the room. Claire hadn't asked what was happening outside this underground bunker, and they hadn't volunteered. That probably meant things hadn't improved.

They couldn't try to bring Falkor into the underground bunker; he was simply too big for it. That created some logistic issues that Claire didn't focus on. She left those up to the FBI. She was busy worrying if she had overpromised what she could do. The thing was, the other two had come back from Prometheus with a gift, but not her. He had told Claire that her will would be her power, which made no sense. She wasn't bending metal or stopping rivers from flowing.

Truthfully, she felt no different, and now she'd promised her team, Falkor, and the FBI that she'd be able to get this dragon across. She didn't know if she could. She'd cut her hand, and then Falkor had opened his flesh beneath his scales, but was that enough blood? Had any DNA actually transferred, and was it useable? Claire couldn't know those answers.

What if I fail? she wondered.

The voices in her head didn't answer this time. They left that up to her, apparently.

During the next few hours, while the FBI rushed to determine where they could pull the dragon over, Claire called her parents. They cried with relief when they heard her voice and begged her to remain safe. She told them she'd do her best. After she managed to get off the phone with them, Remington showed up and gave her the plan.

They were going to bring the orb outside of the bunker

and into a vineyard in the Virginia countryside. They were currently moving military forces there and would have tanks, infantry, and a helicopter above. They were also bringing Jack and Marissa to the field; in case nothing else worked, their new powers would be beneficial. Claire agreed with it all, with one stipulation.

"Don't attack Falkor. He's young, and he might be nervous when he first crosses over, but he won't hurt us. He is on our side, and it's important that all your military men understand that. If you attack him, I don't know what will happen."

A few more hours passed, and then Claire was hustled to the place they'd taken her blood before. "We're doing it again?" she asked the lab technician.

The man nodded as he hooked a needle up to her arm. "Yes," he responded simply.

"Want to tell me why?" Claire sat in a dentist-like chair with her right arm turned so the palm faced up. She winced slightly as the needle pierced her arm.

The tech turned a knob at the base of the needle, and Claire's blood started to flow. "I'm not very high on the totem pole here, but from what I understand, you left a very small amount of blood on the other side of the Veil. Our scientists want to get a bit more to make sure we have enough."

That sounded fair. After a few moments, she asked, "You hear any more about what's happening above? Is it worse?"

The tech paused for a second, studying the needle and tube, then looked at Claire. "I'm not sure how much I'm supposed to discuss, but I hope you can help us. They say you might be the only one who can. There's a lot of people dead up there, and the ghosts have just arrived from Miami. A lot more are going to die."

Claire swallowed. She hadn't realized other people were depending on her, not outside of her parents and now Frank. This tech looked at her as if she held his life in her hands. "I'm going to do my absolute best."

The tech nodded, then returned his attention to the needle. "Then so am I."

They drained blood for a few more minutes, then unhooked Claire. The tech told her it would take about thirty minutes for them to process her blood, and she could wait in this room if she wanted. Claire asked if she could visit Dr. Byron, and the tech shrugged. "Not up to me. Just make sure you're back here in thirty."

Claire found Dr. Byron in his room a few minutes later. The FBI must be extremely busy because no one had tailed her through the halls. Perhaps they simply watched her through the cameras on the ceiling.

She knocked on the door, and the professor answered it a few moments later. "How are you doing, Ms. Hinterland?"

"I've had better weeks," Claire answered. "I've got to go back down there in a few minutes. Would you mind walking with me?"

Dr. Byron looked around his small room. "Well, you're sort of interrupting my *Andy Griffith* rerun marathon, but I suppose I can make the time." He grinned as he stepped out of the room and closed the door. There wasn't a lock on it, not that Dr. Byron would have used it anyway.

"I heard about Frank," Dr. Byron said after a few steps.

"I'm very sorry, Claire. I know what it's like to lose friends in war."

Claire shook her head. "He's not lost, he's a prisoner. A POW. I'm going to get him back."

"If anyone can, it's you. Were you able to get what you wanted over there? Was it worth the trade?"

Claire shoved her hands in her pockets as they took a right down a new hallway. "I'm not sure. There's a chance we are going to get a dragon to join us, and Marissa and Jack got new powers. I... That stupid god said he gave me something, but I don't feel any different. I've *seen* what Jack and Marissa can do. Mine is nothing like that."

Dr. Byron nodded. "Jack came and talked to me for a few minutes today. He said he was granted strength and speed? I didn't ask him for a demonstration, but I believe him. He said Marissa was granted telepathy and telekinesis? I do have some confirmation there, since when they left the bunker today, she said good-bye." Dr. Byron shook his head as if he still couldn't believe it. "In my mind. It was the oddest thing."

"Yeah," Claire agreed. "Both of them got something, but all Prometheus said to me was that my power was my will. First, it doesn't make any sense, and second, I don't know how to use it."

They'd reached the blood-drawing room, and Claire opened the door. They walked in, and Dr. Byron sat on the edge of the dentist's chair. Claire leaned against the wall and folded her arms across her chest. She stared at her feet. "A lot of people are depending on me to do something about this, and I keep barreling forward because I want to help my friends. The truth is, I was counting on getting something from that god. He didn't give me anything. Nothing that I can see anyway, and now I've convinced these people I can pull a dragon across the Veil, and..." She shook her head. "I'm in over my head, Dr. Byron. What if I can't do any of it?"

Dr. Bryon's right leg swayed back and forth from his perch. He placed his hands on his knee and studied his shoes as well. "Prometheus was known for his tricks, as you're aware. It's the primary reason Zeus didn't like him—because he kept getting the better of Zeus. He did something similar when he left you in that dark hallway, from Mr. Teams' explanation. However, the gods, for the most part, keep their word. Prometheus might have phrased it in a tricky way, but it doesn't mean he didn't leave you with something."

Dr. Byron looked at his student. "Claire, if I said I wasn't scared about what's happening in the world right now, I'd be lying to you. It's not the first time I've been scared, and it won't be the last time. The world is a scary place; that's one of the most fundamental truths I've learned over my years here. However, that said, if there's anyone I trust to find us a way out of this, it's you. I'm not sitting here telling the FBI that they're going too far or using you too much because I don't believe it. You're coming into your own now, becoming the leader your psychological profile said you would be. All leaders have doubts from time to time; the key is not to let them pull you away from your purpose. Not to let them paralyze you. Whether or not Prometheus gave you special powers, you're the one who can defeat these Mythers, and I know that for a fact."

Claire looked up at him, still tucking her arms over her chest. "You really believe that?"

Dr. Byron smiled back at her. "I think we all do, Claire. I know Jack and Marissa do. I'm fairly certain Remington and Lance do too, despite their countenance. I've been in touch with Dean Pritcham, and the entire school is waiting with bated breath to see what you do. You're already a hero, regardless of what happens. You're the best mankind has to offer, and those who know you believe you will come through for us without reservations. You can do this, and we all believe you will."

Claire was about to step away from the wall and hug him when the door opened. The tech wasn't standing there, but rather a woman in a white coat she hadn't seen before. "My name is Dr. Chiver. You're Claire, I presume?"

Claire nodded as Dr. Byron stood up. He didn't say anything to Dr. Chiver but instead stepped in front of Claire. He put his hand on her shoulder. "You got this, Ms. Hinterland. Now believe in yourself like we all do."

He turned around. "Dr. Chiver, I'm sure it's a pleasure to meet you, but I should probably be on my way now. Do let me know if you need anything."

And with that, he left Claire alone with a new stranger —one she would shortly find out had information no one could have ever expected.

Dr. Chiver moved into the room and stood next to the chair Dr. Byron had just left. "Claire, I wanted to talk to you a minute before we bring you to the control room. Is that okay?"

Claire hesitated, "Well, I guess it depends on what you want to talk about. If you're going to try to talk me out of what I'm about to do, it's best we just leave now."

The doctor waved her hand. "No, no. What you do is not within my purview to decide. However, I am the person who inserts your DNA into the system we use to cross the Veil, and... Well, something has changed. I've alerted the FBI agents about it, but I also wanted to talk to you."

Claire came off the wall, alarmed. "What is it?"

The doctor studied her clipboard for a second and then placed it on the chair. "It probably won't do any good to show you charts right now, and I'm not sure what it means. Your blood has... Well, it's changed. To be honest, I've been at this for over thirty years, and I've never seen anything like it. If we weren't short on time, I would say it is impossible and demand more tests, but that will have to wait until later."

Claire put her hands on her hips. "Great, now are you going to tell me what's different? Am I dying?"

The doctor's eyes narrowed for a second, then she looked shocked. "Oh, no. I'm sorry. I didn't mean anything like that. You're still healthy. There's no need to worry about dying. It's just... Well, human blood is made up of certain parts. It's the same in all humans, regardless of blood type. Our last test showed you as normal, and now..." Her voice trailed off.

Claire picked it up, "And now I'm less normal?"

She nodded slowly. "Yes, something like that. It appears

something is latching onto your red blood cells, and it isn't a particle or entity I've ever seen before."

"What do you mean?"

The doctor sighed. "I'm not a hundred percent sure what I mean. Something is inside you and multiplying. It's slow. Right now, from the blood we took, only about ten percent of your blood cells have these foreign entities attached to them. However, just in the bit of blood we've drawn, we can see that they're multiplying. They split off from one another, and then they search for another blood cell."

Claire didn't have the slightest clue what any of that meant. She felt fine, but the doctor looked bewildered. "I'm sorry, Dr. Chiver. It's like you're speaking Chinese. Are those things hurting me? Are they killing my blood cells?"

The doctor shook her head, although her face still held confusion. "No, they don't appear to be doing anything outside of multiplying and attaching."

"Wait," Claire interrupted. "Frank crossed over twice. Did you draw his blood the second time?"

Dr. Chiver nodded. "We did," she said, glancing at her clipboard. "There was no difference in his blood. We haven't checked the other students yet, but when they get back, we will."

Claire quickly thought through what this might mean, and in the end, she came to only one question that mattered. "Is this going to stop anything from happening with trying to pull Falkor over?"

The doctor's lips grew thin, but she shook her head. "Assuming Falkor is the new Myther, no. I don't think it's going to interrupt us trying to find him. I must caution you, though, that I don't think it will work. They told me what you did with your hand and the Myther's body, but I don't think that's going to be nearly enough of the DNA we need to locate this creature."

That was all Claire needed to hear. They could figure out what was happening with her blood later, but for now, the decision was simple. They would move forward. "Okay. We can deal with all that when I get back. Right now, can you take me to this command center?"

Dr. Chiver grabbed the clipboard from the chair. "Yes, that's fine. They're all waiting for you."

The two exited the room, and for the first time, Claire realized she had no idea what to expect. There'd been no briefing, not from Remington or Lance, and not from this woman either. "Umm, this is probably a bit late in the game to ask, but what am I going to be doing?"

Dr. Chiver chuckled while turning left down another hallway. "That's sort of the question I posed to the FBI agents. What we're doing here is very scientific and out of our hands once we load the DNA sequence. Either the map, which you'll see, shows us where the entity is, or it doesn't. If it doesn't, there's nothing we can do. If it does, we press a few buttons, and the orb latches onto it. So, outside of watching, there isn't a whole lot you're going to be able to do. Any of us, for that matter. We will either see the entity or we won't."

Great, Claire thought. *Wish someone had told me this before. Maybe if I hadn't been running headfirst, I would have thought to ask.*

"Here we are," Dr. Chiver said as she pushed open another door that looked like all the others in the place.

Claire stepped through and then stopped.

It looked like something out of a sci-fi movie. Fifteen people sat with their backs to Claire, all of them facing computer monitors, some inlaid into the desks. Or rather, there were two rows, each being a single desk. It reminded Claire of what she always thought a NASA control room might look like when they were about to launch a shuttle. The room was darker than the outside hallways, with the lights being dimmed, and the reason for that was obvious. On the far wall was a huge screen that stretched the width of the room, and right now, a single bright, red dot lay in the center.

A man on the right side of the room looked at the new entrants. He was obviously military, dressed in his well-cut suit. Claire hadn't realized the military was running part of this operation, but she supposed for her purposes, it didn't matter. "Dr. Chiver, are we ready?"

"Yes, General Bridger." Chiver folded her arm and clutched her clipboard to her chest.

The general's voice grew louder as he announced to the room. "Begin sequencing."

A flurry of typing began. Claire leaned closer to Dr. Chiver. "What's that red dot?"

The doctor whispered back, "That's the orb detecting you. You see, you're the only person in the world with your specific DNA, so it's only able to see you. We've figured out how to focus the orb on the other side of the Veil, and that's where we hope to see another red dot. Usually we would be looking for you, but this time, we're looking for the Myther you want."

Claire nodded. "Thank you." She took a few steps back

so she was alone and nearly against the wall. She crossed her arms over her chest.

The military man spoke again, his voice loud and commanding. "Proceed to cross the Veil."

More keys were punched, with people leaning in and touching the monitors embedded in the desk. Claire kept her eyes on the screen at the front of the room. The red dot that signified her faded until there was only blackness.

General Bridger took a step forward. "Confirm that we have crossed the Veil."

An anonymous voice said, "Confirmed, sir."

"Continue searching," the general demanded.

There was more typing, but the intensity was less. Nothing was showing up on the screen, just darkness that felt like it would continue forever.

Another anonymous voice spoke from the rows. "It's unable to find the DNA, sir."

General Bridger shot back quickly, "Continue searching."

Dr. Chiver took a few steps back so she was next to Claire. "We should see something. The orb is quick. It doesn't need much time to find what it's looking for. Whatever engineers designed this knew what they were doing."

"So, you're saying it won't find my DNA?"

"It doesn't look like it," Dr. Chiver whispered sadly.

That, Claire couldn't take. First, she liked Falkor. Second, she owed him a debt to help find his family. Lastly, they needed that dragon. Claire gritted her teeth and unfolded her arms from across her chest. Her hands slowly turned to fists.

We need him, she thought. *The world needs him, and I told the world I could do this.*

Claire's skin began to grow hot, her face turning pink, although she didn't notice it.

This stupid machine is bullshit if it thinks it's not going to find Falkor. Claire hardly ever cursed, but as she thought about what was happening, she couldn't help it. *I cut my damn hand open to give that dragon blood, and this machine is going to find it.*

Her body grew hotter, drops of sweat appearing on her forehead and the back of her neck. *You're going to find him, and going to bring him to whatever field Jack and Marissa are waiting in.*

Fury glowed in Claire's eyes, a determination that no one in the room noticed, but that was an unbreakable will.

In the far right corner of the screen, a faint pink dot came into view.

The general practically yelled, "What is that?"

"We have a lock," came the answer. "Commence sequence?"

General Bridger stepped forward as if he couldn't help himself. "Commence!"

The flurry of typing that came next was louder than any of the previous, but Claire didn't hear it. Her eyes had locked in on that pink dot, and she wasn't letting go for anything.

After a few moments, the entire screen went black, and Claire blinked. She finally felt the sweat all over her body and her nails digging into the palms of her hands. A phone was ringing somewhere in the room, but it sounded very distant, as if perhaps it was behind the Veil.

Claire blinked again, still staring at the place the pink dot had been moments before. It was gone, and she didn't know what that meant.

The general picked up the phone. "General Bridger. Yes, sir. Yes, sir. Thank you, sir."

He hung up. The entire room was staring at him.

"Ladies and gentlemen." The general smiled. "There's a huge red dragon standing in a field about a hundred miles from us. Well done."

Cheers rang throughout the room, and Claire's fists relaxed. She turned to Dr. Chiver. "He's here? It worked?"

The doctor was all smiles. "It appears so. You were right. It worked."

Claire felt relief wash over her, although it was momentary. As the cheers faded, the general turned to her. "Please escort her to the dragon. There's much work to be done."

CHAPTER TWENTY

They took a helicopter to the field, the first time Claire had ever ridden in one. She was accompanied by two soldiers, although neither spoke to her after the introductions. As they flew south, away from DC, she was able to see smoke rising from the capital. The destruction of her country, and so many lives lost—even after everything she'd experienced, it was still unfathomable. Like it wasn't really happening.

Claire only needed to look at the rising smoke to convince herself it was.

She forced herself to look away from the dying city. She needed to focus on what had just occurred because she didn't understand it. The orb hadn't been able to detect anything at first, and then suddenly, it saw Falkor.

How? she wondered. The doctor had said it either worked or didn't, but nothing about needing to search. And yet...

Claire remembered what Prometheus had told her. *Your power is your will.*

Then she thought about how her blood was changing. Some foreign entity was latching onto her blood cells, something no one had seen before. Truthfully, in any other situation, Claire would probably have been rushed to the hospital. Now, though, with the world coming to an end, there wasn't time.

The question, which Claire couldn't answer, was whether her desire—her *will*—had caused the orb to see Falkor. Or did it cause her blood inside the dragon to somehow be more visible?

Was Claire responsible for what had happened, or had it been luck?

Quite simply, she didn't know, and that wasn't a good thing, heading into a war.

The helicopter pilot spoke before anyone else. "I can't fucking believe it."

Claire was looking at the same thing—a dragon. The flight had taken about thirty minutes, and Claire had worried whether or not the FBI would listen to her and *not* attack Falkor. From what she saw as the helicopter descended, everything was okay.

The forty-foot-tall dragon was in the middle of the field, his massive tail like a Tyrannosaurus Rex's. His wings were folded back against his body, and his head was tilted toward the machine descending next to him. A perimeter had been formed around the creature, with soldiers and tanks about fifty feet away on all sides.

Claire didn't know how many of the soldiers could see

the creature. She leaned toward the pilot. "Can you see him? All of him?"

The pilot didn't look at her, only nodded. "I've been exposed to these things quite a few times. I see 'em just like you do now."

Claire leaned back in her seat. She saw Marissa and Jack next to Falkor, their heads turned up as well. Remington and Lance were farther back, and neither of them seemed to care about the helicopter. They were still studying the dragon, even after an hour of looking at him.

He really is majestic, Claire thought.

The helicopter finally landed, and Claire hopped off. The rotors were slowing, but the wash was still fairly heavy. Claire reached up to keep her hair from blowing around as she ran toward the group.

Marissa wrapped her in a hug before she could even get to Falkor. "You did it. Remington and Lance told us the whole way over that there simply wasn't enough DNA on the other side, but you did it, Claire."

The FBI agents walked up, both smiling. Remington put his hands up defensively. "Hey, we were wrong." He turned toward Falkor, having to look at the sky to see the top of the dragon's head. "I don't see how we can lose now."

Lance shook his head, clearly still in awe. "Me either. This was smart, Claire. This was really, really smart."

Jack meandered over to the group. "First, it was my idea, I just didn't want to take credit for it. Second, you guys are still in for a surprise."

Claire looked quizzically at Jack. "What do you mean?"

He was grinning his devilish grin. "I managed to

whisper something to our big red friend before these two knuckleheads got here."

Claire's eyes narrowed. "What are you talking about?"

Remington and Lance turned toward Jack. Remington looked like he might pull his weapon on the young man. "Yeah? What?"

Jack looked up at Falkor, still grinning like a madman, and yelled, "Hey, buddy, what's the weather like up there?"

The dragon dropped his head quickly, causing soldiers around the perimeter to raise their weapons. The size and speed caused a gust of wind to move with the creature, and his head came to a stop a mere foot in front of the five people. Remington and Lance had their weapons drawn, fingers on the triggers.

Falkor didn't seem to notice. "It's a bit chillier than down here, I suppose."

Claire understood then and thought it might be the best prank Jack had ever played. She immediately looked at the agents, who had paled. Each slowly lowered his weapon but didn't take his eyes off Falkor.

Lance spoke first. "It fucking talks?"

The dragon slowly moved his head toward him. "I'm a he."

Jack laughed so hard he collapsed on the ground, his hands clasping his stomach.

Without looking at Jack, Remington said, "I'm going to kill you, kid. You nearly gave me and everyone else out here a heart attack."

Without a doubt, Falkor was grinning now. His massive teeth somehow looked both menacing and friendly.

Claire elbowed Lance. "Hey, tell the group to stand

down." They'd heard the dragon, but their weapons were still raised.

Lance nodded and managed to pull himself away from the creature. He turned toward the perimeter and grabbed a two-way radio from his belt. "Stand down. There's no threat. The fucking thing talks."

Claire watched with relief as the perimeter weapons began to drop. Jack finally got up, still chuckling. "You can't blame it all on me. Sissy here knew what was happening. She didn't tell anyone either."

Marissa was smilingly sheepishly. She shrugged. "Couldn't help it."

Remington holstered his piece. "I'm going to arrest both of you when this is done. Now, we need to figure out the next steps, and I don't think this creature is going to fit in any building the FBI has. Jack, since you've been busy using all that brainpower to play tricks, maybe you've got some advice on where to keep this thing?"

Remington had been kidding. The FBI did have a plan ready in case Claire managed to pull the beast over, although when they saw his sheer size, it seemed inadequate.

"Not going to work," Lance said, and Remington had to agree. New plans were quickly drawn up, and like it or not, more time had to be spent. They finally decided the only place they could house the dragon was the university, and they asked Falkor to fly to it above the clouds so as to not freak out anyone who might be able to see him.

A plane took the students back, another bringing Dr. Byron. The agents came with the students, although they were on their phones the entire time. Claire gave them space, knowing they were trying to figure out what came next. You had two students with powers never before seen, a freakin' dragon who could breathe fire, and...

Well, me, Claire thought. She didn't know how she would fit into the plans, only that she'd helped already. The new powers for her friends, Falkor... *And all it took was sacrificing Frank.*

Claire shoved the thought away. She knew she was going to get him back, come hell or high water.

Everyone arrived back at the university, and Dean Pritcham nearly lost her mind, trying to keep the students from all filing out of the building to look at the dragon housed in the yard. It was agreed that for the next day or so, only Claire's group and the agents would have access to him. The dean also was worried about how to feed the thing, but when she met him, he simply said, "I'm a dragon, not a pet. I'll find food."

Dean Pritcham eyed Falkor. "No humans. Understood?"

The dragon grinned. "No humans. Yes, ma'am."

It took the FBI another twenty-four hours before they all met. They did it outside the funhouse. The agents, the dean, Claire and her group, and Dr. Byron wandered out. No one said anything; he was a part of the core group.

Of course, Falkor was at the meeting as well.

They'd set chairs out in a semicircle facing the dragon. He was lying down, looking lazy in the grass. His eyes were closed as the agents started speaking.

Remington began the outdoor meeting. "How much

have you heard about what's happened since you all crossed over?"

Jack had a nail file out and was using it on his right hand. He didn't look up. "Not much. You want to know what I figured out, which old Prometheus forgot to mention? My nails are basically like iron now, and this stupid file won't work. Clippers either."

Dean Pritcham looked like she might hit him, but Remington kept going as if he hadn't said anything. "The ghosts now hold DC. It won't be our focal point for now."

"Why? What's going on?" Claire asked.

Lance leaned forward in his chair. "The gods are on a rampage. They apparently plan on destroying the entire east coast. They and their group have moved through Baltimore and appear to be heading for New York. We imagine it's going to be New York City. If their current path of destruction holds, they're going to hit it tomorrow evening just before dusk."

Jack, still acting nonchalant, pocketed his nail file. "I think you could probably just put me up there by myself. Have it fixed in an hour or so." He yawned, although his grin almost broke through.

Remington scratched his chin. "I'm serious about arresting you when this is over."

"For what?" Jack asked. "Saving the world?"

The agent shook his head. "Somewhere there are laws about how annoying you are. I'm sure of it." He leaned back in his chair and looked at the dragon, who appeared to be snoozing. "Falkor, you listening to me?"

The dragon didn't open his eyes but mumbled, "Trying,

but you humans prattle worse than any creature I've ever heard of."

"Just keep listening," Remington demanded, although not with the same edge he used on Jack. Perhaps a few metric tons of muscle calmed one's voice. He leaned back in his chair to address the whole group again. "We've gone over this multiple times within our ranks, and there doesn't seem to be any way we can launch a sneak attack. Our red friend here isn't going to help with stealth, especially when he starts breathing fire. More, Ares' birds will see him coming."

Lance shook his head and looked at the grass. "We can't give you any real support. Our military is futile against those two. Hell, Hades hardly even attacks. He just lets the other one go on insane rampages."

"So," Remington continued, "the best minds in the world have come up with a simple plan of attack. We're going to beat them to New York City, and that's where we're going to have our war."

The agents leaned back in their chairs simultaneously, obviously waiting for the critiques.

Claire had mostly been quiet so far, and for the moment, she was content to let her team speak. She looked first at Marissa. "Thoughts?"

Marissa crossed one leg over the other and stared admiringly at Falkor. "I don't see any other way either. It's not like we can go through the sewer system and pop up as a surprise." She looked at the agents. "It would have been nice if we could have stopped them before they got there. What's the city like now?"

Remington answered, "We were able to evacuate a lot of

the citizens, more than anyone actually thought possible, and that's working against the gods. There have been a lot of deaths, though, and a lot of wreckage. We'll brief you in a more detailed fashion before we get there."

Claire turned to Jack. "And you? Without your theatrics, please."

Jack waved away her barb. "My theatrics are what help you get through your day. Look, honestly? I'm ready. I owe Hades an ass-kicking for what he did to me last time, and now I've got the tools to do it."

"Falkor?" Claire asked. "Any thoughts?"

The dragon turned his head to get more comfortable. "Sooner, the better."

Everyone was in, at least from her squad. She supposed the academics had opinions, but they weren't shy about voicing them if they disagreed, so Claire would take their silence for agreement. "I guess that settles it, then. We'll meet them in New York tomorrow evening. Is there anything else we should know?"

Remington shook his head, frowning slightly. "No. The city is surrounded by our military, and other militaries from around the world are offering assistance, but all of our weapons are ineffective. Invading with troops will just mean a lot of humans die."

Lance stood up. "Well, I'm liking these powers and dragon you brought over. This is the shortest meeting I've had with you people and the one with the least amount of arguing. You'll have all your briefing materials tomorrow morning."

Claire didn't like that. "Why tomorrow? Why not tonight?"

Marissa placed her hand on Claire's knee. "Tonight, we should probably call our parents and..." Her voice trailed off, but Claire got the gist. Tonight they should probably enjoy themselves as best they could.

Because tomorrow, they would fight gods.

CHAPTER TWENTY-ONE

Hades heard the witch enter behind him. His chair was turned so he was facing the window, and what a view it was. For the first time, he sort of envied Zeus, because his brother had seen views like this nearly his whole life. Hades sat on top of what was called the Empire State Building. He didn't know why they called it that, but he liked the term empire, so this was where he'd retired. From here, he could see all the vast buildings of this wonderful city. Sure, there were dead in the streets and fires raging uncontrollably throughout multiple buildings, but none of that concerned him at the moment. No, all of that would be taken care of in due time.

What concerned Hades was the witch. "Yes? What were you able to find out?" He didn't turn around to look at her.

She remained at the door. "They will be here tomorrow."

Hades spun his chair around. A vast oak desk sat in front of him—a "businessman" used to own it, although he didn't know what that meant. The terms didn't matter in his world, and shortly, they would not matter in this one either. "Are you sure?"

The witch had used her sight under Hades' direction to try to understand what the girl was doing. She'd been mostly unsuccessful until now, and the witch hadn't been able to give him a real reason.

She remained at the doorway, obviously not wanting to venture too close to the god. "Yes, I'm sure. I can see her and her friends. They're at the university."

Hades stroked his chin. Cerberus was sitting across the room, one pair of eyes open. He hadn't moved when the woman entered since he understood she wasn't a threat. "It perturbs me that you haven't been able to see her until now. It perturbs me greatly. You still have no idea what had happened?"

"I don't know why I couldn't see them, but something has definitely changed with their group."

Hades stopped stroking and raised his eyebrows. "Are you going to tell me, sorceress, or stand there looking stupid?"

"They have what appears to be a dragon with them."

Hades stood, dropping his hands to his sides. Cerberus hopped up, looking for possible danger. The god leaned forward and placed his hands on the desk as he eyed the witch. "Think about what you saw, woman. Think about it hard, then tell me again what you just said."

Concern grew on her face, and she took an involuntary step back. "I-I-I've never seen a dragon, but that's what I think it is."

Speaking slowly and still leaning over his desk, Hades directed, "Describe to me what it looked like."

The witch obviously didn't know why the danger in this room had increased so quickly, but she felt it the same as the dog. She closed her eyes and took a deep breath, then let it out gingerly. "It was red. Huge, like the size of a house, or even bigger. Its tail was long and easily the width of an old oak tree. Its skin is red and scaly. I didn't see it fly or anything, but I saw wings layered over its back."

Hades straightened and walked to the front of the desk, shortening the space between him and the witch. "In the time you saw the dragon, did it happen to be eating any of them? Or burning their little university to the ground?"

The witch shook her head but remained silent.

"Pray tell, dear. *What* was the dragon doing?"

The woman swallowed as her hands slowly crept into her pockets. "It looked to be sleeping while they were making their plans." She paused as if unsure of what to say. "Th-the dragon is theirs, I think. I don't see any other way to interpret what I saw."

Hades spat on the floor, flames dancing in his eyes. "Dragons belong to no one, certainly not a *human*. You're going to do two things for me. The first is to get out of my sight, and the second is to find Ares and tell him to come here."

The witch didn't need any other instructions. Indeed she looked relieved to get these. She pulled her hands from her pockets and quickly skittered out the door.

Hades turned so he could look out the window again. This was not good. This might actually be *bad*, and that wasn't something Hades had thought possible until now. Was it right? The prophecy? Was this dragon a harbinger of destruction the stupid girl would ride in on?

Hades didn't know, but dragons were nothing to trifle with.

He heard the door open again but didn't turn around.

Ares' voice sounded lackadaisical as he spoke. "I admire how much you can scare that poor woman, Uncle. I think she might have pissed her pants once she ran from my office." He stopped a few feet from Hades' back. "What do you want?"

Cerberus had padded over and was licking Ares' hand, but when Hades spoke, the dog whimpered and backpedaled a few feet.

"They have a dragon," he told his nephew.

"Who?" Ares asked. He took a bite of something, and Hades finally turned around. The god was eating an apple.

"*Who?*" Hades almost exploded with rage. "The people you've been brought here to kill. The students, you dolt! That witch just told me she has seen them, and they're coming tomorrow, and they have a *dragon*."

Ares shrugged while staring at the apple and chewing. "These apples might be better than the ones on our side." He looked at his uncle. "Have you had one?"

Hades shook his head in disgust. "No wonder my brother hates you so. You are perhaps the most undeserving god in our entire family."

Ares rolled his eyes and took another large bite of the red apple. He walked past Hades to the windows overlooking the city. "Are you scared of a dragon?"

"Scared?" Hades choked out. "I'm immortal. I cannot die. Win or lose, there is no reason for me to fear anything. Am I worried that flying hellfire might stop us from winning this world? Yes. Have you ever faced a dragon in battle?"

Ares turned around, one eyebrow raised. "Have you? Have you ever *been* in a battle?"

Hades placed his hands on the desk and leaned forward. "Who do you think banished the titans, boy? Did you think it was Zeus? No. I was right beside him in that war, so don't try to act like the god of war is the only one who knows violence. Now answer my question. Have you ever faced a dragon?"

Ares once again rolled his eyes and then turned to look out the great windows. "Dragons, titans, gods, humans— they're all the same. Perhaps some can't die and must be banished, but it matters not in the end. They can bring this dragon, and I will destroy it as I have everything else in this world."

Hades shook his head in disbelief. This god was a fool. "Boy, they are not like other creatures. They rule the skies in a way Zeus *wishes* he could. And another thing you might not be fully grasping right now—how did they *get* the dragon?"

Ares started to say something but stopped.

Hades nodded at the younger god's back. "Exactly. From what I understand, they don't, or didn't, have the ability to pull through the Veil. And you at least know those beasts aren't friendly to those not their kin, so if they *could* pull from the other side, how did they pull a dragon and *not* get burned alive? It leaves only one option, which is even worse than the dragon."

"What's that?" Ares asked.

Hades' eyes narrowed. "You cannot be this stupid. I

refuse to believe it. The only other option is that they *crossed* the Veil. That they met the dragon and somehow *tamed* it. I wonder what else they were doing over there? Perhaps getting powers like the five morons here have? Maybe Zeus has somehow co-opted them, and we'll be facing his power tomorrow. Maybe—"

"Stop it." Ares turned around, and the look on his face caused Hades to straighten up. It was pure hatred, not the lackadaisical young man who'd wandered into the room moments before. "If you don't want this war, why did you start it? That is *my* question. If you don't want to win in glory and drag their bodies through the streets below, go home, Uncle. Go back to your underworld and wait for this to be over. And if you can't cross over, then please leave this city, because I cannot handle hearing you complaining right now. The witch says they come tomorrow? Then tomorrow they die, and we inherit a new world. One untouched by the other species who try to rival us for supremacy. We inherit a world of weak creatures who will do our bidding or die. So let this dragon and its minions come. I'm ready to take what is mine."

Ares dropped the core on the floor, held his uncle's eyes for a few more seconds, and then walked toward the doorway. He stopped just before he exited. "Do not call me with this prattle again. Tomorrow we go to war, so bring that fancy little hat of yours, and please don't squeal at the sight of a little spilled blood."

Hades heard the door shut. A smile slowly spread across his face. The omens weren't great right now, but despite his nephew's stupidity, the girl was in trouble when she arrived.

CHAPTER TWENTY-TWO

Their last night at the university wasn't normal, but it wasn't bad either. They made their calls to their parents, and tears flowed. Turned out the other students had organized a going-away party, and it also turned out what they had planned had broken the dean's rule for it. Sam dragged the three out to the field where Falkor was housed, and the entire place was lit up and had tables full of food, and even a banner stretched across two trees.

HAPPY BIRTHDAY!

Marissa had looked at it and crooked her head to the left. "I don't think it's anyone's birthday."

Sam laughed. "Yeah, but we had all of an hour to get this stuff set up. Someone found the layout online, and I ended up printing it."

Claire had put her hand on Sam's shoulder, smiling and looking at the banner. "Thank you. Sincerely."

Somehow a few of the kids had snuck in some alcohol, but no one got too rowdy, and Claire was glad for it. Her group didn't drink, not even Jack, which shocked her. Made her proud, too, and she told him that.

"Look," Jack had responded while holding Sam's hand. "Tomorrow I'm going to be out there with you two nitwits, and I'm gonna need every bit of my brainpower to think us out of the trouble you two get us in."

Marissa had punched him in the shoulder, then the two left him and Sam to hang out alone.

Eventually, Dean Pritcham was alerted and sauntered down with security guards. She'd taken a look at everything, standing thirty feet away from the big bonfire Falkor had lit. After a few minutes of staring at the students and the students staring back at her, she'd simply said, "Don't fuck up."

With that, she left the group to their fun.

Claire knew she and her group needed to get some sleep—or at least to try to. She was standing at the edge of the light the fire cast, and she thought she was alone. She nearly jumped out of her skin when Falkor's huge head came down next to her.

"Goodness!" She stepped back. "How the hell do you move so quietly?"

She couldn't see one side of Falkor's head, and he appeared to be looking at the students around the fire. "I've seen you humans shrug. I wish I could do that right now. You seemed to be in pretty deep thought."

Claire's heartbeat was slowing and she stepped back to her spot, crossing her arms over her chest.

"Have you been in a battle?" the dragon asked.

Claire nodded without looking at him. "Quite a few times. This will be the biggest, though. Have you?"

"No," Falkor whispered. "This is my first time."

Claire hadn't realized that. Everyone was so afraid of dragons, it was like they hatched from their eggs having already been in battle. She looked at Falkor. "Are you scared?"

The dragon was quiet for a time, but Claire kept looking at him. She was still the leader of this group, and since Falkor had joined it, she was his leader too. She needed to know how he felt going in as well.

The dragon spoke softly. He knew his deep voice could carry easily, but he clearly didn't want others to hear him right now. "I think *who* we are fighting is more important than the fact that we're fighting. If it was any other creature, I don't think I would worry. Ferociousness is in dragons' blood. We were born to do battle. There is no other reason for us to breathe fire." He stopped talking for a moment and looked pensively at the bonfire. "I wouldn't be here if I didn't want to find my family. I'll admit that much, at least. Those creatures tomorrow—they are the gods of old. They can't be killed, only banished."

The dragon spoke as a youth who hadn't fought yet, but Claire sensed an older soul inside him. A wise one. He was scared, but he knew his inherent power and felt a duty to his kind. Claire moved over next to the dragon's massive head and touched him just above his neck. "You know I beat him last time, right?"

The dragon's left eyebrow raised. "Really?"

Claire left her hand on the creature's body. "Yes. A few months ago, we faced Hades down and beat him. I went there to get my friends back, and as you can see from this party, I did that. Frank, too. He's gone now, and I've got to get rid of those gods so I can go back and get him." She patted his head and then took her hand away. "I guess I'm just saying it's okay to be a little scared. Understand also that if I had to choose between saving Frank and saving the world, I don't know what I would do. Truth. That's how much Frank means to me. Luckily, I don't have to choose. I have to save the world to get to Frank, and that's a whole lot of incentive."

The dragon slowly raised his head off the ground, then his neck. He stared at the bonfire for a few more seconds and then looked down at Claire. "Thank you."

Claire nodded and smiled, staring up at the majestic being. "Get some rest. Tomorrow we save the world and all that jazz."

The dragon gave a slight nod and turned away. Claire watched him walk into the darkness, shocked by how quietly he moved when he wanted to. Falkor couldn't do anything about the footprints he left behind, though.

CHAPTER TWENTY-THREE

Claire wouldn't remember much of the next day. The morning, afternoon, and even much of the flight to New York were a blur. Maybe she had breakfast, maybe she watched Sam give Jack the first kiss anyone had ever seen them engage in. Maybe Jack turned red, and when Marissa ragged him, he told her he'd gotten a sunburn from the bonfire the previous night.

Maybe that didn't make sense, but they all let it go.

The day leading up to the battle was a prolonged period of acting like they weren't doing what they were doing. They joked and ribbed each other. It wasn't until they reached Falkor that their façade faded.

How did we ever ride him any other way? Claire wondered silently.

The dragon was now equipped with a saddle of sorts. Remington and Lance stood at the feet of the beast, looking up as Claire and her group arrived. They had their hands on their hips and were staring up with smiles on their faces. "Not too bad, eh, Claire?" Remington asked.

Jack spoke before she had a chance. "How the hell did you get that thing created in such a short time?"

Claire was wondering the same thing. The device attached to Falkor *could* be considered a saddle, but that didn't do it justice.

Lance turned around to look at Jack. "It wasn't that hard to do. We took some measurements on Falkor here, then had the good doctor in the basement work up something we could throw on top of him. Here, look." He turned to Falkor. "There are three seats, one for each of you. You can strap yourself in and not have to worry about falling out if you hit turbulence or Falkor needs to do a barrel roll or whatever. Bottom line, you're safe to fly."

Jack walked up to the dragon and put his hand on what looked to be a pocket. "And this?"

Remington stepped back and opened his arms wider. "We've taken the liberty of packing for you all. Jack, I looked for your toothbrush, but couldn't find it. Apparently, you don't brush."

Jack was already rummaging in the pouch. "Hardy-har-har." He pulled out Marissa's book of spells and turned around to show it to her. "Think this might help?"

Marissa started toward him, curious about what else they might have. "Certainly can't hurt."

Claire followed her group while Falkor waited patiently for them to rummage through the saddle he now wore.

"Go to the other side," Remington instructed.

Claire followed his directions and went to the first pocket she saw on the far side. She reached in and immediately knew what she was holding—the baseball cap that made her invisible. She hadn't thought about the thing in ages. She turned around with a smile on her face. Remington was standing in front of her. "I thought it might come in handy."

"Thanks," Claire said as she looked down at it. "It probably will." Her smile faded as she realized she would need it more than anyone else. The others now had innate powers that would help them. If she did, well—

Remington interrupted her train of thought. "I know what's going through your mind."

She raised an eyebrow and glanced up. "Oh yeah?"

"You think I put that in there because you don't have super strength like Jack, and you can't move things with your head like Marissa." Claire was about to say something, but Remington raised his hand to stop her. "No. There isn't time to argue with you right now. I just wanted to let you know I talked to Dr. Chiver last evening. You remember her?"

Claire nodded.

"She told me about what happened when you pulled Falkor over. She wants to run some more tests when you get back, and I told her it would be up to you. I did ask why she wanted to, though. Know what she said?"

Still holding the hat, Claire shook her head.

"She told me about your blood, but truthfully, I don't understand. What I did understand was that she told me when the orb was searching for Falkor, based on everything she knows, it was impossible for the orb to see him, and then suddenly he pops up on the screen. That room you were in? It was wired with cameras, and she told me that she's rewatched the video quite a few times."

Claire's eyes were narrow. "Rewatched what?"

Remington nodded toward her. "You. She watched what happened in the room, and she said the only change, right before Falkor's light showed up, was you. Your hands turned to fists. She could tell you were gritting your teeth."

"Yeah. I was pissed. I thought we weren't going to get him over."

Remington smiled. "You're as stubborn as ever. Anyway, I didn't give you that hat because you don't have powers. I gave it to you because I want you to have everything you can at your disposal to defeat those bastards." He paused for a moment. "You've got some kind of power, at least according to Dr. Chiver. Just be ready to use it when it's time."

Remington said nothing else, just walked back to the other side of Falkor, leaving Claire holding the hat alone.

"All right," Dean Pritcham called from the far side. "It's time to mount up and get going."

Claire shoved the hat back into the pocket and pulled the flap down. She trotted over to where the group was. Jack was holding his impaler. "Remember this?"

Claire smiled. It seemed like a lifetime ago when they'd used that against Dracula.

Lance stepped up. "You all read your briefs this morning?"

Everyone confirmed they had.

"You know the plan once you arrive?" he asked.

Everyone affirmed.

Claire's eyes caught something moving in the distance, a lone figure coming into the field from the university. She knew who it was immediately—Dr. Byron.

They turned as he approached, and Jack spoke first. "Got a speech to give us?"

Dr. Byron looked surprised like the idea had never occurred to him. "I'm not one for talking, Mr. Teams. You know that."

The whole group laughed, even Lance.

Claire looked behind her at the dragon. "Can you see him, Dr. Byron?"

The professor wetted his lips silently as he looked in the same direction as Claire. He nodded very slowly, although his face betrayed no emotion. "I can. I finally can."

Falkor turned his head toward Byron. "Name's Falkor."

"Byron," the professor responded, staring at the dragon's teeth. "It's a pleasure." He stared for a few seconds and then tore his attention away. He looked at Jack. "I didn't come down here to talk to you all. I glanced out the window and thought I could see the creature, so I sauntered down here to see if I could. And I can. I'm tired of talking to the likes of you anyway." He smiled warmly at the jab.

Jack smiled back and stepped forward, wrapping his muscular arms around the older man. Dr. Byron looked shocked for a moment, but when the other two joined in, he wrapped his arms around them as well. "It's been a pleasure for you three as well," he said.

"Even me?" Jack asked through the maze of arms.

"Most of the time."

Remington stepped close to the group. "Okay, okay. We've got to get going. They'll be back by this time tomorrow, and you can all hug then."

Jack smiled broadly. "By then, my name will be known

from sea to shining sea and then some. I'll be charging for hugs."

Claire slugged him in the arm, then rolled her eyes and looked at Falkor, who was staring down at the group.

"You humans are interesting. Now, would you mind hurrying it along? I haven't eaten since last night, and I'd like to see what god tastes like as soon as possible."

The dragon circled New York City, flying above even the skyscrapers. Dusk had set in, and there looked to be a storm coming in as well. Claire had a rendezvous planned with the military personnel in a few moments, but she'd asked Falkor to show her the bird's eye view first.

Claire didn't know much about New York City. She knew what was in the movies, TV shows, and what the FBI brief told her. Even with such a small amount of knowledge, what she saw beneath her took her breath away.

Fires blazed in the streets, and more burned in the windows of the glorious buildings the city was known for. This was all from an extremely high vantage point, but she needed to see more. "Can you take us down closer?"

Marissa called, "Won't it be dangerous? We can't fight back."

Looking down at the city, Claire responded, "Don't care. I want to see."

On his next turn, the dragon started descending. He went slowly, looping around until they were flying below the skyscrapers and between buildings not quite as high. Tears filled Claire's eyes as she looked at the disaster below. She didn't know New York, but she knew people, and she knew what she now saw meant the devastation of countless lives. Cars were overturned on the streets, and fires burned throughout the city. On two different streets, she saw people fleeing from one building to another like rats. A few stopped and looked up at the flying creature, and Claire felt sure they saw Falkor. Something had happened here to the ones who hadn't been able to leave in time. Their brains had changed to allow them to see Mythers.

Their lives were clearly still in danger.

Claire saw dead bodies beneath her, some face-down on the pavement and some staring up at the sky as if they longed for a savior. But none had come.

I can't save everyone, she thought, *but I can save those still here.*

"Okay," she said to Falkor. "Take us up and then to the rendezvous point."

The dragon was quiet as his wings hoisted them higher into the air, a miraculous creature that now flew over a devastated city. Claire didn't need to look back at her friends to know how they were feeling: at least as horrible as she, and perhaps more because they had both visited this grand city before.

It took them a few minutes to make their way to the meeting zone. It was just outside the metro area in a now-deserted parking lot. New York's backdrop and skyline were easily visible, just a mile to the bridge that had once taken traffic to and from the city that never sleeps.

Hummers covered the parking lot, and the buildings had been commandeered for military use. As the dragon descended, flapping his wings hard to soften the landing, men in Army fatigues came to help the students down.

Claire waved her hand at them. "No. We've got to be able to do this by ourselves." *Wish we had more practice*, she thought but did not say.

It wasn't hard to get down. Each seat was equipped with a rope, and they simply threw it over the side and then slid down—carefully, to avoid rope burns.

"Welcome," the first soldier said to Claire. "My name is Lieutenant Drexler. My men and I are here to offer as much support as we can."

Claire extended her hand, and the man took it. "We've been briefed. Thanks for coming."

The soldier looked at the city behind her and shook his head. "I only wish we could do more."

"Can you see the creature behind me?" Claire asked, stepping aside.

"Yes, ma'am," Drexler answered. "All the men and women here have been transferred to this unit because we can see Mythers. The other bases we have set up on the New York City perimeter can see them as well, although some of them have military members from other countries. It was necessary to ensure we had enough people."

Claire felt odd, the way the man was speaking to her. It was like he held her in high esteem—all of them, actually. The FBI had always treated them like students, but now for the first time, they were being treated as leaders. *Doesn't hurt to fly in on a dragon, I suppose.*

The soldier pointed toward a long plastic picnic table about thirty yards away. "We've got everything set up over there, including gear that will help you locate the targets."

He looked at Falkor but kept talking to Claire. "He's going to need to be careful not to hurt anyone."

The dragon was staring at the table. "I will be."

The color drained from Drexler's face. "He talks?"

Jack patted the man on the shoulder. "It's a thing. You'll get used to it. On the bright side, Falkor won't need to walk over to the table. His eyes and ears are about ten thousand times better than any human's, so we won't need to worry about the tail breaking anyone in half."

Falkor snorted at the clumsy remark but said nothing.

The soldier nodded, clearly struggling to regain his wits after hearing a dragon speak. Everyone walked over to the picnic table.

Claire looked at it quickly. A map of New York was spread across it, with red circles drawn in a few places. Soldiers stood by the table, but all of them had their eyes glued to the dragon. Drexler glanced around. "Gentlemen, these are the students."

Everyone's faces swiveled to Claire's group, and once again, she saw respect in their eyes and in the way they moved. These people saw Claire, Jack, and Marissa as saviors, not as kids or students. Sure, they had a dragon, but the respect was for them, the fear for Falkor.

"I won't introduce everyone since we're not central to your mission," Drexler continued. "Our weapons, as you're aware, are useless against this enemy. Even our air support won't do much but destroy more of our buildings. You understand?"

"We do," Claire responded.

The soldier nodded and then looked at the maps. "Now, all our scouting reports show that the Mythers and human assisters are moving between these three buildings." He pointed to three circles on the map. He stuck his left hand out, and someone handed him a red Sharpie. He uncapped it and wrote Humans on the building farthest south, then drew an arrow pointing both directions between the first and second building, then the second and third. He wrote Ares above that and drew a line connecting him to the arrows. Finally, in the building farthest north, he wrote Hades.

He nodded as he looked at his work. "That is pretty much what we're looking at. I know it's crude, and might not be what you're used to, but everyone is short on time."

Jack shook his head as he read the map. "Nope. This is about as good as we've ever seen. Maybe even better."

Drexler continued speaking. "The humans don't move around a lot from what our aerial surveillance shows. They, after the initial invasion, remained inside this building you see here. The same for Hades, only that's on the northern side of this line."

He looked up at them almost expectantly.

Claire looked at Marissa and Jack, who returned her gaze, then focused on Drexler again. "Okay. You said something about equipment?"

"Yes, ma'am." The soldier leaned down and brought up a plastic box, which he placed on the table. "Now, none of this is super high-tech or weapons." He nodded at Falkor. "That creature back there is probably the greatest weapon you'll have. These things here are to help you stay in contact with one another and to help you locate the targets regardless of the lighting."

He pulled out three earpieces and placed them on the

table. "One for each of you, although we've been told that one of you might be able to communicate without it."

Marissa opened her mouth to say something, but the soldier waved.

"No, ma'am. I apologize, but our clearance only involves a certain level. We haven't been given specific information outside of that, and I'm not sure it matters for our purposes. Regardless, all three of you should have these earpieces. They're Bluetooth- and LTE-connected, so regardless of where you are in the city, you'll be able to communicate, both incoming and outgoing."

He didn't pause but pulled out three pistols in holders next.

"These are standard issue nine-millimeter Glocks, nineteen plus one in the chamber." He pushed the guns over to the students. "I'm sure you're aware, but I want to remind you, these are not for the Mythers. They don't even work on the birds Ares controls. However, there are still people in the city, and while we want to save everyone we possibly can, right now, our first objective is to defeat the Mythers. If any humans try to attack you or otherwise disrupt your mission, these will work on them. They'll also work on the five humans inside."

Claire thought about Al, the ghost. "Do you know if there's a sixth inside? The witch we captured and then Hades took from the compound?"

The soldier nodded and looked to his left. A man about two inches shorter stood at attention immediately. Without offering any information about himself, he stated, "We do believe there might be a sixth. Aerial photos have shown what appears to be a woman, but there isn't any confirmation on that."

Claire nodded. She knew she'd need to talk more with Jack, Marissa, and Falkor, but one thing was clear in her mind. "I need everyone who is supporting us, all the other encampments like this, to understand that if they see any humans exiting, they aren't to be hurt. I don't know what's going to happen, but the witch needs to be kept alive for now if at all possible."

"Yes, ma'am, that's understood. We have confirmed sightings of the Mythers and also understand that some of the humans might have the ability to shape-shift. All humans exiting will be detained unless they are an immediate danger."

That was the best Claire could hope for. She looked at the box again. "Okay, let's continue."

The soldier next pulled out three pairs of glasses, or that was the closest thing Claire could compare them too. Perhaps they were more like goggles, but not quite. The lenses appeared slightly darker than normal eyeglasses but not as dark as sunglasses. The frames were thick, both vertically and horizontally. "These are state-of-the-art. They're lighter and can give you more information than the older models." He pressed a button on the right side. The glasses darkened. "This button flips the glasses between night and day vision. They darken like this to protect your eyes in case you accidentally turn them on when there is enough light to see or someone turns on lights in an already dark space. The natural shade of the glasses will help keep glare out of your eyes during the day as well. The lenses are ballistic-grade bulletproof. A grenade frag won't crack the glass. More, there are LIDAR cameras built into the frames. Same technology they use for self-driving cars."

Jack, clearly unable to help himself, asked, "Did Musk build these?" He grinned.

Drexler looked up without a hint of a smile. "No."

Claire shook her head. "I apologize. I can't even be mortified by his antics anymore. Let's continue, please."

"What?" Jack asked, still smiling.

The soldier picked up the glasses and turned them from side to side. "What this does is assist you with peripheral vision. If something comes up on the side, you'll see an orange dot on that side of the lens. It'll help your reaction time."

Marissa reached forward but stopped just before touching them. "May I?"

The soldier pushed them into her hand. "They're yours."

Marissa smiled and put them on her face. She turned around so that her back was toward Claire. "Come up on my left."

Claire took a step forward so that Marissa couldn't possibly see her, but she was easily in an attack position.

"Oh, yeah." Marissa smiled. She turned toward the table while taking the glasses off. "Definitely going to be hard to sneak up on us."

The soldier nodded and pushed the other two pairs of glasses toward the guns already on the table. He turned around and pointed at three large bags behind him. They were camouflaged and had many different pockets. "These are standard-issue backpacks. In case you have to be in there for any length of time, they're loaded with non-perishable food and water."

Claire's eyes narrowed as she studied them. After a moment, she made her decision. "We're not taking them. They're too heavy and will only slow us down. If we're in there for any length of time and need food, then our dragon is dead, and we're probably not coming out either."

The soldier turned back around and stared at her for a few seconds. "Yes, ma'am. That said, this is the support we can offer. I wish we could do more, but we've lost a lot of men already, and while we are willing to fight, our superiors have said we are to see what happens with you all. You're our best hope."

Claire might have said something meaningful, but Jack didn't give her the chance. "Don't sweat it, boys." He slapped each of his biceps with the opposite hand. "This here is Thunder, and the other is Lightning. It's a storm those gods over there are going to wish they had never gotten caught up in."

Marissa groaned.

Claire sighed. "I'm sorry, gentlemen. Truly."

Falkor's booming voice broke the spell of Jack's ridiculousness. "Humans, I'm hungry, and there are gods to eat."

While Claire and her crew were speaking with the military, Ares was putting his armor on. He had seen the dragon flying in the sky, not needing his birds to whisper of it. He had watched as the dragon swooped low over the city of

New York. An arrogant creature to be sure, but Ares liked that. He had been called arrogant too.

He was in his uncle's tower, and he knew Hades had seen the overgrown lizard as well. Hades had just picked up his shield, now prepared to walk outside and begin battle, when his uncle entered his room.

Hades closed the door behind him. "You saw the dragon?"

Ares looked at his spear in response. The bloodlust was on him now, the joking gone.

Hades nodded. "I won't be on the battlefield with you, but I am going to be assisting. The human minions and I aren't going to face them head-on. That is your job. Understand that we will attack when the moment is right."

Ares banged the metal part of the spear against his shield. The sound of metal on metal echoed through the room. "Fight or flee, it makes no difference. I haven't eaten roasted dragon before, but I plan on it tonight. I wonder what it will taste like."

Hades smiled, although Ares didn't care about his approval. He was the god of war, and the war was now starting.

Hades stepped to the side, clearing the way for Ares. "When we finish them, we'll need to deal with Zeus since I have no doubt that he is aware of what's happening."

Ares ignored the older god. He was ready to kill.

Hades watched his nephew leave the room. The creature truly was something different. He cared only for war, only for blood; the politics of situations didn't concern him. He had so much confidence in himself that he didn't even consider he might lose to this girl. Hades was fine with that.

It served his purposes very well.

If Ares thought he couldn't lose down there, he would fight as hard as possible. For Hades' part, he wondered if Zeus' fear had been prescient. Perhaps this girl was special; after all, she'd found a dragon. Hades had seen it this morning, flying through the city as if *it* were the ruler rather than the god of the underworld. Maybe she was *supposed* to be fated to stop the invasion, but Hades had to hand it to his brother—he had thought the plan through.

Ares was no one to trifle with. He would fight harder and deadlier than Hades could. And when he lost? The girl would be weakened. Her dragon would be weakened. Her friends would be weakened. Hades would step in and finish them all, and then he would look at Zeus and smile. This world would be his.

CHAPTER TWENTY-FOUR

Perched atop Falkor's back, Claire saw the first building in the row of three. Judging space was hard from this high up, but it appeared to be about a half-mile away. "Falkor, I want you to land on the road. Drop us off there, then provide aerial support. Understand?"

The dragon glanced down to see where she wanted to go. "Just make sure you stay out of the way when I breathe."

Claire's eyes widened at that, unable to tell if the dragon was joking. Even if he was, it didn't mean he was wrong. It was not like the flames shooting from his mouth were a laser. The dragon began a circular descent, not dive-bombing to the ground. It took a few minutes, but they eventually landed just about where Claire had instructed.

The dragon laid down so that the dismount would be easier. The three did it efficiently and silently. Jack already had the impaler strapped to his waist, along with stakes to reload. Their guns were holstered to them. Marissa had left the *Book of Shadows* with the military, explaining she knew the spells by heart. All three wore their glasses, and Claire was certain they would come in handy, given that the sun was setting on the horizon.

Claire's hat was strapped to her belt.

After they'd all hit the ground, Falkor stood back up. He looked down at Claire as she circled around to his front. "I haven't seen the gods yet. They haven't come out of their buildings."

Claire nodded and peered down the road in front of her. She could see the first building from where she stood, the one that housed the humans. They would deal with them first and move forward from there. Without looking up at Falkor, she said, "We'll be dealing with hand to hand combat a lot, I imagine. Can you support us without burning us up?"

Falkor raised his snout to the sky. "Don't worry about me. Just try not to die. I want to see my family again."

Without another word, he let his haunches drop, then leapt into the air, his wings giving huge pumps as he took flight. Claire and the other two took their eyes off their immediate surroundings to watch him depart.

Still staring at Falkor, Marissa commented, "I'm going to be sad when he goes back across."

Jack scanned the buildings around him, starting to scout. "To hell with that. I'm going to convince him to stay. He's much cooler than a Tesla, and he's going to be my ride whenever I pick up girls."

Claire raised an eyebrow. "You mean Sam?"

Jack waved away the comment, then his face grew serious. "This is really the end, isn't it? All this time has led us to here, and now we either win or lose."

Claire glanced at Marissa and saw the same feelings mirrored on her face. All three were carrying the same weight—the weight of the world. "It is the end, but for them, not us. Let's go."

Claire started walking down the street. She knew their final destination, although not what would present itself on the way—but that had been the case the entire time, hadn't it?

On her left, she saw a small girl and her father peer out of a broken window on the third story of a building. The girl's face was covered in soot and dirt. The father had his hand on her shoulder. Neither said anything, most likely too frightened to give their location away. *Do they understand we're here to save them?* Claire wondered. *Or are they too frightened right now?*

Jack's voice cracked through her thoughts. "Up ahead."

Claire's head whipped forward, and she saw what he meant.

"That's some getup he's got on," Jack quipped as he stepped farther to the right of Claire. Marissa did the same thing on the left, assuming the formation that would give them the greatest advantage.

Claire had seen the god on television, but this was different. He was maybe three hundred yards in front of them, having stepped out of a random building onto the street. He walked with his right shoulder to them until he reached the middle, then turned to face them. A sword was strapped to his back, the handle poking up over his shoulder. A shield resided on his left arm, and his right held a spear. He wore a helmet that covered much of his face, making him look even more menacing. He was tall, his body lean, and his armor protected all the vulnerable parts of his body.

Claire stopped walking, the other two doing the same.

Jack called from ten feet away, "What's the plan, Stan?"

Claire looked into the sky. Falkor was up there, circling around, waiting for her to move. His dragon eyes could see everything perfectly down here. She turned her attention back to the god. "Plan is we go up there and beat his ass. Jack, you're going to have to take the lead. Marissa, you support him with your new powers."

Jack grinned. "What are you going to do, Your Highness? Sit back here and give orders?"

Claire unclipped the hat from her waist. "If you two do your job, he won't even see me coming." She placed the hat on her head. Ares was too far away to judge his reaction, but when she glanced at Marissa and Jack, she saw familiar looks of surprise on their faces. She was invisible to them, but they could still hear her. "Let's go."

Jack smiled. "That is one ridiculous hat." He turned toward the god, his smile falling away. "Sissy, how far can your mind work?"

A few seconds passed before she answered. "I'm moving small pebbles to where he is now without much effort."

Jack nodded. "Good. I'm going to sprint from here."

Claire started walking forward. "I'll be coming in behind you, Jack. Marissa, you get in that sweet spot where you're most effective with your mind, but far enough out so as not to get hurt."

Marissa started forward as well. "Got it. I'm going to move a little farther in for better control."

"On your mark, Jack," Claire instructed.

Jack took a deep breath, then screamed, "*FOR SPARTA!*"

Claire couldn't help but grin at his goofiness. Jack took off, and Claire's smile died. He was so fast. Faster than anything she'd ever seen or believed to be possible. Her feet paused momentarily as her brain lost track of what she was doing. "He's like the damn Flash," she whispered.

Jack was halfway there when the spear flew through the air at him. Claire still hadn't taken another step.

The spear looked like it was going to split Jack's head in two, but he moved just in time, and the thing raced by him. Claire's head turned to watch it go, flying by her at nearly the same speed Jack was running.

When Jack reached Ares, he dropped slightly lower and leapt upward, slamming into him and sending them both flying.

Claire looked at Marissa, who was staring in amazement. Neither of them did a damned thing to help. Claire had to get them both snapped out of this brain fog. "Marissa, we gotta get down there!"

Marissa said nothing, just started running at full speed. Claire did too, her feet swiftly separating her from her friend.

She watched as Jack and the god fell back to the ground. Ares hit the ground first, with Jack on top. The asphalt cracked beneath them and they skidded down the street, Ares' armor creating sparks until they came to a stop. Jack's fist was slamming into the god's face over and over. After a moment, he grabbed Ares' helmet and threw it into the air.

Claire saw the god's face for the first time then. He was smiling as blood dripped from his lips. Jack paused as he stared at the wicked grin, clearly understanding how much this creature was enjoying the battle.

That slight pause gave Ares an opening. He grabbed Jack by the ribs and thrust him upward. Jack flew backward, the god's strength obviously matching his.

Marissa focused on him. His descent should have been quick and harmful, but as his fall started, his body turned so that his feet faced the ground and he slowed. He landed easily about twenty feet from Ares and kept his eyes on the god. "Think you can do that?"

Ares had climbed to his feet. His shield had been dislodged when Jack hit him, and it now lay discarded on the sidewalk. "Hades was right. You did get powers along with your dragon." He chuckled while reaching up with his hand to wipe away the blood trickling from his lip. He looked down at it. "Not bad." As he focused again on Jack, his right hand smoothly unsheathed the sword from his back.

He moved forward with incredible grace. Jack grabbed his impaler and shot a stake at the god. It should have hit him in the face, but instead it disintegrated, just as the bullets had. Ares stopped in mid-stride and laughed. "The weapons from this planet are nothing to me, boy. You've been given a gift with your hands, but nothing else shall strike me. Use your hands, and let's see who is better."

Jack stood frozen for a moment, understanding washing over him. "A little help."

When Claire felt wind coming from above, she knew what it meant. "*JUMP BACK!*"

Jack did as she commanded, and just in time. His leap took him into the air, and Falkor swept down on Ares. The god turned his attention to the dragon too slowly, and the flying beast grabbed him in his giant mouth.

The three watched as the dragon flew back into the air, carrying the Myther with him. Claire and Marissa rushed to Jack's side as Falkor ascended.

Jack screamed into the air, "*KILL HIM!*"

The god struggled, his sword stabbing into the dragon's snout. Blood splashed Falkor's face. A tremendous whine escaped from the dragon's throat, sounding like the most horrible dog yelp ever.

"We've got to help him," Claire said, still invisible amongst her friends. "Marissa, can you do anything?"

Before Marissa could act, Falkor released the god from perhaps a hundred feet up. Ares fell as the dragon continued his flight upward. Gouts of blood trailed the god down. The dragon turned slowly in the air, pointing his massive jaws toward the ground again. Fire rushed from his mouth and engulfed the falling god, continuing past until it slammed into the ground.

The flames spread in all directions, heading toward them at a rapid pace, pushed by the dragon's incredible lungs above. Jack wasted no time. "Claire, to me, now!"

Claire jumped next to him so he could feel her. He grabbed her with his left arm, and with his right, took hold of Marissa. He ran as the fire came for them, not caring who it burned on its destructive path.

He was too fast for it—too fast for anything but the god now roasting in the flames. Jack came to a stop and put them both down. Claire took the hat off as they turned to look. Falkor had flattened and was now flying the opposite way down the road.

"Is that the end?" Jack asked. "Did Falkor kill him?"

Marissa shook her head. "He's getting up."

Claire stared at Ares, trying to see what Marissa could obviously feel with her mind. The fire was dying since its source was gone, although the road in front of them still burned hot enough to keep them from moving closer. Claire saw a slight movement beneath the flames, something rising from the pavement. "There." She pointed. "Marissa, you know what to do."

Marissa took a step forward and closed her eyes. The street was a wide one, and all kinds of things had been abandoned on it. An overturned car, a truck with its bed separated from the front part of its body. Trash and overturned trash cans, plus innumerable pieces of glass. Claire didn't know if they were usable as weapons against the god, but she hoped Marissa's power would somehow allow them to harm the being.

That was Marissa's thought too. She closed her eyes and set her jaw. The trash cans littering the street lifted first. Some burned as they hovered in the air, but none moved forward; Marissa was getting control of her weapons. She picked up the glass next; thousands of shards rose off the ground simultaneously. Claire watched it all, mystified by what her friend was doing.

Finally, Marissa lifted the vehicles. In all, there were four—two on this side of the flames, and two behind. All four became weapons.

Ares was standing in the middle of the flames. He peered out at the three. The fire didn't allow them to see his damage, but clearly it hadn't been enough to put him down for good. None of the three could approach him, not with the fire burning so hot. Even from this distance, beads of sweat covered Claire's face and arms.

"Do it," she commanded Marissa. "Do it now."

Marissa was sweating badly from the heat and the mental effort of holding all that weight up. She nodded, brought her hands out to her sides, and then threw them forward.

Everything rushed toward the god as if he were a black hole sucking it all toward him. Glass, metal, even beams Claire hadn't previously noticed soared through the air.

Ares must have seen them coming, but he didn't move. He held his sword in his hand, fire burning across his body, and simply waited.

He didn't have to wait long.

The objects collided with bone-crunching force. The sound of metal and glass smashing into each other filled the street and echoed high off the buildings. Marissa remained in front of Claire, her arms holding their pose in front of her body, hands clasped together. The flying objects now crunched and ground against the creature in the middle, none of them dropping, all trying to crush Ares.

"He's too strong," Marissa whispered harshly. "It's not going to kill him."

Claire's eyes widened. "Jack? Can you do anything?"

He shook his head. "Not with that fire. It'll burn me alive."

Suddenly, the makeshift weapons that were all trying to crush Ares lowered. "He's kneeling," Marissa explained.

Claire understood what was happening before it did. "GET DOWN!"

Claire fell flat to the ground, her chin touching the asphalt as she stared forward. Everything that Marissa had sent toward Ares rushed back out at them. It came with the same speed and the same force, ready to annihilate them as they'd tried to do to him. Jack hit the ground second. Marissa barely made it, a metal beam passing where her hips had been a moment before.

The god rose and walked forward, ignoring the flames and the injuries he'd sustained. Claire climbed to her feet slowly, as did her friends. The god's skin was raw, and half his face had been destroyed. His armor had large punctures where Falkor had bitten down, and blood leaked from the holes. He walked with a limp, his left foot dragging behind him, yet he was still coming. Claire and her group had sent everything they had against the creature, and he was still coming forward.

Marissa stepped back. "What do we do now?"

A voice came from behind Claire. "I suggest you die with dignity."

Claire whirled, already knowing who was there. Hades. He stood a block away, his voice booming across the empty space. In front of him were the five cult members, all of whom had powers. Claire recognized how vastly outnumbered they were. Even with Falkor, wherever he'd gone now, there were six versus four.

Jack was on edge as he spoke. "Claire, not sure if you've noticed, but we're sorta trapped. You got any ideas to get us out of this?"

The dragon's voice boomed from overhead before she could answer. "GET INSIDE!"

Claire was staring at the five as the words reached her

own ears. Their eyes had turned to the sky and they momentarily froze, but Claire knew what was coming. She took off to her left, desperately hoping to find an open door or window. Jack was faster. He swept her up as he passed, already holding Marissa in his arms.

The flames rushed behind them. Jack kept running, lowering his shoulder into a wall and bursting through it.

Claire heard screams from outside, knowing what they meant. Perhaps the gods could survive Falkor's flames, but the humans could not. Jack set them down, and they turned around to see. Flames roared across the road outside, some having even ventured inside the building. Claire could feel the heat baking off the street, even from this far away. Jack started walking forward, but Claire grabbed him by his shirt. He turned around, his face asking why she stopped him. "Not yet."

She was right. Ten seconds passed, then a fresh batch of flames roared down from on high, this time coming from the opposite direction. Falkor had turned around and come back, roasting the earth for a second time. The human screams were gone, and Claire heard nothing else. She didn't remember which one of them had been able to teleport like Frank, but perhaps that one had made it out alive. She doubted anyone else had, however—no one human, at least.

"We're stuck," Marissa said. "It's going to take a while for those flames to die down, and even when they do, we won't be able to walk outside. The shoes will melt off our feet."

Jack faced them. "Not trying to put any more pressure on ya, Claire, but we're running out of ideas, and I don't think we have a whole lot of time to come up with more. Tell me you've got something inside that head of yours."

The voice boomed again from outside, the god of the underworld calling for her. "Girl, where are you? I'm still here, but I don't see you anywhere. Did your dragon burn you away as he did my minions? I was hoping you would put up a bit more of a fight."

Claire gritted her teeth. The flames were fading some on the road, dying down without the necessary fuel to feed them.

"Come out and play, girl," the god taunted again. "Stop hiding."

Claire looked at Jack, then Marissa. Both of them were staring at her.

Marissa shook her head. "No, you can't. You won't survive out there, Claire. It's too hot. Even if you could beat them, that fire will melt your skin."

"Listen to me," Claire said. "You two find the stairs in this place. I don't know how high the building is but get to the top of it. Jack, carry Marissa up there. Get Falkor's attention or a helicopter or something else, but you two get out of here. If that son-of-a-bitch wants me, he can have me."

Jack laughed. "You're kidding, right? You're not actually going out there alone?"

Claire looked at the broken window that led to the street. "Find the stairs and get to safety." She started forward and immediately felt Jack's strong hand on her shoulder.

"You can't. You'll die. If any of us go out there, we die, Claire. We all just tried, and we failed. Even that damned dragon failed. We've all got to get to safety and then regroup. Find another plan. Find another way." Jack pointed to the street. "Out there is death, and you know it."

Claire turned and looked at him. "Get up those stairs because I'm going outside. You both get to safety. Now. It's my last order to you."

Jack opened his mouth to say something but realized it wouldn't matter. He could try to pick her up and carry her up the stairs with him, but that wouldn't matter either. She'd find a way around his strength and his speed. Claire wasn't taking no for an answer, and what was he going to do now, stop listening to her? "You're my friend, Claire. You're my leader. I don't want to leave you here, and I know Marissa doesn't either, but if that is what you demand, then that's what we'll do."

"I'll see you both in a little bit." Claire said nothing else. She simply pulled out of Jack's grip and started walking toward the street. After a few seconds, she heard footfalls as Jack and Marissa found a staircase. The door they went through closed behind them, then she was alone. She kept moving forward through the ruined building. The flames were dying down outside, but she still felt the heat.

Claire removed the hat from her waist once again, but this time she didn't put it on her head. She let it fall to the floor. She was done with gimmicks. Done with weapons. She'd face those two demons masquerading as gods by herself, and either she would win or lose, but she was done with the rest of it.

She reached the shattered glass windows and looked to her left and right, finally seeing both of the gods. Ares was to her left, and he looked like death. His armor was black, with flames still rolling across parts of it. His skin was raw, and his eyelids were gone. He held his sword, although it was as black as the rest of his armor. Claire turned to see Hades. He wasn't nearly as badly off as Ares, but he wasn't in tip-top shape either. Fire had licked his left sleeve and burned the right side of his face, yet he must have had some sort of protective shield that kept it from getting to him.

"There you are," Hades mocked. The two gods started walking toward each other, meeting in front of the building she stood inside. Claire could feel the heat baking off the street, and it made her fearful of going outside. Every cell in her body wanted her to remain where she was because Marissa had been right. Jack had been right. Death waited outside.

The gods stopped twenty feet from her in the middle of the road. Flames danced around both of them, but they ignored them. "You hurt my nephew," Hades said with a sick smile. "I think he wants vengeance, don't you?" He turned his head to the wrecked god. Ares grunted and took a step forward on his right leg, his left dragging behind it.

Your will is your power. The words came back to Claire as Ares struggled forward. His speed and fluidity gone, he now looked like a zombie trying to find brains to eat. *Your will is your power.* That was what Prometheus had told her.

What did she want?

"My damn world back." Claire stepped through the shattered window. The heat immediately tried to swipe at her, and her body wanted to acquiesce and go back inside the building. *No,* she thought as she stood on the sidewalk. She looked up and saw Falkor flying above, but he wasn't descending. Perhaps he understood what she was doing.

Sweat beaded on her forehead and arms. Ares took another halting step forward, pulling his left leg behind him. Fire danced on Claire's left and right, and a flicker of flame reached up to touch her pants. She looked down at it, feeling calm. "No," she told it. The flame paused as if it had heard her speak and was unsure what to do. "No," she told it again, and the flame *listened*.

It retreated back down the trail it had taken to get to her and remained there, not daring to come forward again.

Claire turned her eyes back to Ares. He was perhaps five feet away now. He didn't seem to notice what she'd just done, or if he had, he didn't care. His eyes were full of hate and bloodlust. He raised his sword, and Claire turned toward him as he did. Before he had moved like some kind of spectral knight, but now Claire saw him as nothing more than an insect. "No," she whispered again.

Ares' sword paused in mid-swing, his eyes narrowing. He grunted; it was obvious he was trying to bring the sword forward, but it wouldn't move. Claire walked toward him, crossing the distance until she was next to him. She raised her hand and put it on the blackened armor. "Goodbye."

Claire shoved, and it was as if she'd taken all of Jack's strength and then some. The god flew backward, slamming into the building across the street but not stopping there. He broke through glass, concrete, brick, and metal, disappearing from Claire's view. She turned to Hades then. The god who had killed so many, who had destroyed city after city, stared at her with his mouth slightly open.

He took a step back. "It's not over, girl."

Claire heard the growl of his dog on her left. Cerberus, the three-headed hell dog that would eat her as soon as look at her. Claire didn't bother turning to him. She took another step toward the god. "It's over, Hades. Don't you see?"

The dog barked at her with all three heads, but it sounded fearful. He wasn't rushing forward but keeping a safe distance between him and Claire.

She smiled. "Even your dog is scared, Hades." Another step forward and Hades matched it with one backward. "This isn't your world, Hades. It's not any Myther's world. This place is for humanity, and I want you gone. You, all your ghosts, and anyone else you brought over here to hurt us."

Hades unsheathed his spear from his back. "You don't command me, girl. You're a mortal, and I will live forever. Now stand back."

Claire heard the patter of claws as the dog lunged forward, obviously fearing for his owner's life. Claire turned toward him, and the dog stopped in its tracks. Four feet from her, he lowered himself to the ground, all three heads lying on the sidewalk. "Good boy." For some reason, Claire didn't want to hurt this dog, despite the terror and pain he had caused. She looked at Hades, understanding that it was the owner's fault.

The god was staring at his dog, obviously unable to believe he had been cowed by another creature.

"There's nothing left for you here," Claire continued as she took another step forward. "Your human servants are all dead. Your warrior..." She pointed to the massive hole that Ares had disappeared through and shrugged. "I don't think he'll be back any time soon. It's time for you and everyone who came with you to leave. Do you understand?"

The disbelief on Hades' face changed in less than a second. A twisted, angry look took over, and he raised his spear, then thrust it forward with a rage and strength that should have propelled it straight through Claire's chest.

She saw it happening as if in slow motion and raised her hand, placing it directly in front of the spear's path—finally understanding what Prometheus had meant. Right now, her will was all that mattered when it came to Mythers. She didn't know if that extended to the rest of the world, but it didn't matter. Neither this god nor any other creature that crossed the Veil could hurt her right now. The spear should have destroyed her hand, splitting tendon and bone alike. Instead, its sharp point stopped as it touched her palm, not drawing so much as a drop of blood. Hades' arm flexed as he tried to shove it farther. Claire simply moved her hand down, taking the spear with it. The god's struggles were no longer relevant.

"This isn't possible," he spat. "You're a mortal. You cannot stop me. You cannot hurt me."

Claire looked at the sky. Her skin was flushed, red flowers blooming on her cheeks. She was perspiring again, although not from the heat any longer. She felt nothing outside her focus. "Go home," she whispered as Hades continued to curse at her. "All of you. Go home."

Lightning flashed across the sky. She continued staring upward, knowing what she wanted, and knowing that was all that mattered. Another bolt struck, and then another.

Hades was screaming now, but Claire couldn't hear him. She was seeing the Veil ripping apart above her, white spider webs spreading across a darkening sky. "Go home," she whispered again. She held the tip of the spear in her closed hand and closed her eyes as a bolt of lightning touched down directly in front of her.

Two things came to her at once then: an impenetrable darkness and peace.

CHAPTER TWENTY-FIVE

Claire opened her eyes, although she had no idea what she was looking at. Above her, she saw a canopy of trees, and beneath her back, she felt pine needles and rough rocks poking through her clothes.

She felt exhausted, as if she could sleep forever.

Claire coughed and then turned over on her side. She was on a dirt trail of some kind, but she didn't recognize it. "Marissa?" she called. "Jack?"

There was no answer. Slowly, she climbed to her feet, feeling wobbly. *What happened?* she wondered. *Where am I, and how did I get here?*

Both in front of and behind her was a trail with trees on either side. She didn't know which way to go, and she realized she didn't hear any birds or animals. These woods were silent. She had no memory of coming here or of what had happened before she woke up. The last thing she remembered was telling Jack and Marissa to find the stairs and escape. She had been about to go fight the two

Mythers, but she couldn't remember what happened after that.

"This way, girl." The voice boomed from Claire's left. It sounded like the heavens themselves were speaking to her, commanding her to come down the trail.

Claire followed the voice, unsure where she was going but seeing no other option. Even as she walked, she felt she could sleep for days, such was her exhaustion. After a few minutes, the trees parted and she stopped walking, stunned. She had been in a forest, but when she looked in front of her, she realized the forest hung in the sky. Before her was thirty feet of red clay and then a drop-off that ended in the color blue and puffy clouds.

Where am I? she wondered, forgetting about the exhaustion seeping into her bones.

A man sat near the drop-off, his legs dangling over the edge. He had long white hair, and Claire could see part of his beard hanging over his chest. His arms were padded heavily with muscle. "Do you know who I am?" he asked without looking over his shoulder.

Claire blinked, not sure what to be more in awe of—that she was on a world that floated in the sky or that a man was dangling his feet off it. "You're Zeus?"

"Bingo," he responded. He reached up and stroked his beard but still didn't turn around to look at her. "You seem to have beaten me at a game I've been playing for a very, very long time. I'm not very happy about it."

Claire suddenly felt cold. She couldn't remember what had happened before she ended up here, but she didn't think she held a lot of power in this place. "Did I cross the Veil again? I must have. Either that or I'm dreaming."

The god chuckled, his deep voice booming across the sky. "No, you're not dreaming, girl. You're on my side of the Veil, and apparently, what happens to you is up to me."

Claire stepped forward, although she didn't venture to the edge. She remained about five feet away from the god. "Why? If I won, why am I here? What's happening on Earth?"

The god scratched his knee distractedly. "Prometheus played a dangerous game with you, girl, although you didn't know it. The power he gave you wasn't without its negative side. He allowed your will to dominate ours, at least on your side of the Veil, but when you used it, you weakened yourself tremendously. What you did shouldn't have happened without the technology I sent over. However, you were given the power of the gods, so you ripped open the Veil and sent most of my kind back across. You would have died except for the dragon. He swooped down and grabbed you before he was sucked across, and now..." He raised his arms up to indicate his world. "Here you are."

Claire shook her head. "I don't understand. Why am I okay over here but not on my side?"

Finally the god looked over his shoulder. "You feel tired, yes?"

Claire nodded.

"That's the effect. The power you were given was too great for any mortal to wield, but over here, the negative effects aren't as strong."

"Why?" Claire asked.

Zeus looked back toward the sky. "The power originated from here. The farther away from the source it gets, the more you have to stretch to use it. Right now, you're only tired. If you were on Earth, you'd be dead."

"How did I get up here?" Claire asked. "If Falkor brought me, why am I here?"

Zeus picked up a small pebble sitting next to him and tossed it into the sky. Claire watched it fall until she could no longer see it. "I had to bargain with the creature, which isn't something I like to do. Dragons are stubborn and dangerous creatures. Ares finally learned that lesson from what I can tell, although I don't feel bad for the bastard." He chuckled to himself. "That dragon really did a number on the god of war. Hades, too, but not quite as bad. Right now, he's stomping around in the underworld, cursing at every soul that dares cross his path."

Zeus picked himself up off the ground, brushing the dirt from the white toga he wore. He faced Claire, his full glory on display. He didn't hold the danger that Ares had, or the wickedness of Hades, but rather a regality both lacked. "I asked the dragon to bring you here because I wanted to meet you face to face, although I had to promise you both safe passage. Falkor is nearby, and if I don't give you up to him, he'll try to burn this whole air island to the ground."

Claire was more than a little confused. "Why did you get him to bring me up here? If you're not going to kill me, what's the point of me being here?"

Zeus smiled. His teeth were large and white, and his smile disarming. "I just wanted to get a look at you, girl. I have waited for longer than you can imagine to try my hand at taking Earth, and I wanted to see the person who stopped me."

Claire didn't trust this creature. With the flick of his wrist, he could toss her from this island and he wouldn't feel bad about it for a second. "So, what's next? I don't imagine you're going to stop trying to take over my planet."

The god walked away from the edge, careful not to get closer to Claire. Perhaps he could tell she was scared, or perhaps he thought Falkor was watching him from somewhere. "Of course I'm not going to stop. I want that planet, and eventually, I'm going to have it. You see, there are things happening that you don't know about. The Titans, for one. They'll soon be back here raising hell, trying to take what is mine. Earth would allow me to avoid them, at least for a while. So yes, I do plan on having a go at it again."

Claire put her hands on her hips. "So, nothing has changed."

Zeus chuckled. "Oh, I wouldn't go that far." He peered at her for a moment. "You really don't remember anything, do you?"

Claire said nothing, not wanting to give this creature any more information than he already had.

Zeus shrugged and kicked a pebble. "You almost died, not because of what you did to Ares and Hades, but because of what you did to the Veil. You closed it. It's not tearing anywhere now, except in one place. You created a single door."

Claire shook her head and dropped her eyes to the ground. "That doesn't make any..." She was about to finish her sentence with the word "sense," but then it clicked. She looked at Zeus. "And you can't rip it open anymore?"

With a grim smirk, the god shook his head. "No. You've

managed to stop that as well. Whatever you did, my orbs no longer work, and even if they did, the five who followed me are dead now. The only place that opens for the Veil is already being manned by your planet's war-force, which I think you call a 'military.'"

Claire's eyes glazed as she thought about what he was saying. Did the Veil have a Customs check now, the same as when someone entered another country? A smile crept over her face at the thought, because that seemed like the best idea. There were good creatures on this side of the Veil. Mythers like Frank and Al and Falkor. She didn't know how it would work, but she wanted it to be possible.

Frank. The name came to the front of her mind, and her eyes refocused on the god. "Where's my leprechaun?"

He chuckled. "You are a feisty one, no doubt about that. You made your deal with Prometheus, to get powers to defeat me, and in turn, you gave up the leprechaun. Am I right about that?"

"Almost," Claire responded. "I didn't make the deal. Frank did, but it came to the same thing. Now, where is he?"

"You certainly had a lot of irons in this fire, girl," Zeus responded. He turned around and looked off the island, staring at the world below. Claire didn't approach the edge, not willing to risk Zeus tossing her off. Still, she couldn't help herself when the god pointed his finger below. "Here he comes now."

Claire's eyes widened and she stepped forward, her heart full because Frank was coming back. Sure enough, she saw him. A large griffin was carrying Frank on its back, the leprechaun holding on for dear life from the looks of it.

"You see," Zeus continued, "Falkor also let me know that you had made him aware of the trick I played on the dragons." Zeus shook his head as he watched the griffin approach, a sad smile on his face. "I truly had thought this all out, and keeping the dragons hidden during this war was necessary. All anyone has to do is look at what happened to Ares to see that if they had joined humanity's side, we wouldn't have had any chance. Just one of them did all that damage; imagine if it had been a hundred."

The griffin was maybe three hundred yards away now.

"Anyway, your dragon was about to just start burning things when I made a deal with him. If he told me where Prometheus was, I'd give him his family—"

Claire interrupted, "You didn't kill them?"

"Ha!" Zeus laughed loudly. "Kill a family of dragons? You think too much of me, girl. I used magic to trap them while I hatched my plans. The magic wouldn't have lasted forever. Indeed, two years was stretching the limit of what I could do. However, I made a deal with the dragon that if he gave me Prometheus, I'd give him his family back. He's a young one and didn't realize I didn't have a whole lot of bargaining power, given that sooner or later, the dragons would break out anyway."

Frank was almost here, and Claire couldn't take her eyes off him. He had a pissed-off look on his face, and his small fists were gripping the griffin's feathers something fierce. "Why did you get him back for me, then?"

Zeus was still smiling. He'd nearly arranged for the entire world to be obliterated, all so he could have another place to dominate, yet he seemed like a genuinely happy guy. "Your dragon friend told me there wouldn't be any deal without getting the green fellow back." He shrugged. "It wasn't a big deal. Prometheus caused me to lose a war I'd been plotting for centuries, so stealing his good luck charm back isn't that big a deal to me. Happy to do it, really."

The griffin landed on the air island, and Frank wasted no time sliding off. "Ye damned flea-infested beast, I'd rather fly coach on Spirit Airlines than ride with ye ever again." He made a show of brushing his clothes off, then looked at Claire. "I'll deal with ye in a minute."

Frank stepped around the griffin, who wasted no time flying off the island. The leprechaun walked up to Zeus, having to turn his head to look the god in the face. "Ye don't remember me, do ye?"

Zeus put his hands on his waist, still grinning. "Can't say I do."

Frank's expression was just about as pissed off as Claire had ever seen it. There wasn't any joking in the leprechaun now. "Well, remember me now, Zeus. Ye and yer little war had me trapped in a hole for I don't know how long. Ye almost got me killed. Ye almost got me friends killed. Ye had me play nice with a dragon, ride a griffin, fight ghosts and witches and more than I even care to mention. I don't care how powerful ye are, how many birds ye command, or how many lightning bolts ye can shoot out yer arse. If ye ever consider bullshit like that again, I'm going to kill ye."

The god was chuckling, seeming to not care about Frank's anger. For the leprechaun's part, he didn't seem to care about Zeus' laughter. He turned his rage on Claire next. "Now for ye." He stomped over and was just about to start talking when everyone felt the dragon's wings pumping air toward them as he came in for a landing. "Damn it!" Frank shouted. "He's interrupting the damn speech I've been thinking about for hours."

The dragon hit the ground, shaking the floating island. He didn't bother looking at Frank or Claire for the moment. Falkor's eyes were trained on Zeus, and Claire saw real fury in the animal. "I gave you Prometheus." Heat flowed from his mouth as he spoke. "Now, where is my family?"

Zeus wafted his palms toward the ground. "Calm down, my friend. Calm down." He raised an arm and pointed toward the sky in the distance. As he raised his finger, what appeared to be nothing but blue sky and white clouds began to fade. It was as if someone had taken an eraser and was removing paint from the sky. And beneath it?

Claire shook her head. "You're a real asshole. I rarely curse, but there's no other word for it."

Another island sat in the sky, although it was much bigger than the one Claire stood on. That one was the size of a small country back on Earth, with a massive mountain in the middle of it. Forests sat at the base of the mountain, spreading to the very end of the island from what Claire could see. Zeus had trapped the dragons there for two years. The girl couldn't see details since the island was too far away, but she saw creatures begin to soar from the mountain. More and more took flight as they realized their prison had been opened.

Falkor was staring up too, and Claire couldn't imagine how happy he was after so long. He would be seeing his family again shortly. The dragon looked down at Zeus, hatred in his eyes. For a moment, Claire thought the creature might try to burn the god as he had Ares, but then Falkor's attention went back to the sky. Still staring up, he said, "Claire, it was an honor. If you ever need me again, you know how to find me."

Claire was going to say, "Not really," but the dragon took off before she had a chance. His wings pumped, air-tossing her and Frank's hair. She watched as her battle friend went to rejoin his family, all of them streaking back to their home. Claire returned her gaze to Zeus. "You're not worried they will want vengeance?"

Zeus chuckled again and shook his head. "Gods don't worry, girl. They might want vengeance, and they might try to battle me, but that's part of life. There will be more wars, of that you can be sure."

Frank moved closer to Claire. "I'm not done with you yet, just so ye know."

"I'm well aware. One thing at a time, though." She narrowed her eyes as she stared at the muscular god. "And what about Earth? Are you going to keep trying to take over our planet?"

Zeus put his hands behind his back and leaned forward, stretching his spine. He yawned as he did. "Of course, of course. This isn't over, but..." Finishing his stretch, he shrugged. "Earth still has you, and I'm pretty sure Prometheus' little gift isn't going to wear off any time soon. You'll need to be on your guard, but for right now, girl, you've won. You and your little green friend here should take some pride in that."

Frank stepped forward, as angry as a disturbed hornet. "You don't tell me what to take pride in, old man. Now, I want to get back to Earth, and I want to do it now. Are ye going to teleport me over there, or am I going to kick yer big arse right off this island?"

Zeus laughed—not maliciously but happily, and Claire found herself unable to hate the god. Hades, Ares—there had been an evilness to them that permeated everything, but that didn't seem to be the case here.

Don't forget that he just promised to try to take over Earth again, she told herself.

Zeus eventually quit laughing. "Listen, green one, I can't send you back and forth anymore. There's only one area in both our worlds that will allow you to cross. If you want, I'll send for the griffin again, and he can take you there."

Frank shook his head in disgust. He pointed at Claire. "This is her fault. This whole thing. I would almost rather be in that hole with Prometheus then flying on that flea-infested stork."

Claire cocked her head sideways. "I thought you liked griffins?"

He made a fist and thrust his thumb behind his shoulder at Zeus. "I don't like anything that works for him." He turned back around. "Come on, get us the hell out of here. I'm tired of this side of the Veil."

Claire smiled, unable to help herself. "You're coming back with me? You want to stay on Earth?"

Frank raised a finger. "First, it has nothing to do with *ye*. Earth has better beer." He raised another finger. "Second, sounds like I can cross back and forth as I please now, so if ye or them FBI dummies annoy me, I can pop back over here."

Claire reached down and hugged her friend. Frank immediately started grumbling and telling her to let him go, but after a few seconds, he slowly wrapped his arms around her too. "You know I was coming back for you, right?"

"I knew ye were, lass," Frank whispered. "I never doubted that for a second."

"Good."

"Enough, enough," Frank grumbled as he pulled away. "Ye be having me tearing up here soon, and I won't go back to Earth looking like a bumbling idiot."

Claire's smile faded as she looked at Zeus. "Go ahead and get us that griffin."

Zeus snapped his fingers, and she heard one squawking as it appeared in the distance. She didn't take her eyes from the god. "Behind all your smiles and good cheer, I know there's a conqueror's spirit in you. I know you'll come again for Earth. You might think we got lucky this time, but I actually think you did. It was luck that Hades came through instead of you since he was the one who took the brunt of my force. Think about that next time you start plotting, Zeus. As long as I'm alive, I'm going to be ready for you. And the next time you try to come through, it won't be a truce I set up. You understand?"

Zeus gave her a broad smile. "We shall see, girl. We shall see."

EPILOGUE

The world didn't snap back into place immediately, but who could expect that? Across the east coast of the United States, multiple cities had been burned and countless lives lost. The President had been killed, and a lot of other politicians as well. The world, and especially the USA, was a very different place than it had been before the Veil.

World leaders squabbled over what to do about the hole in the Veil that Claire had created and then left. Some pleaded with her to close it, while others begged her to remove the entirety of the Veil. To simply let the two worlds coexist as one. Claire, for her part, ignored both these requests. She'd set up what she desired, and now the world could figure out how that would work. She didn't remember doing any of this; she couldn't remember anything after grabbing hold of Hades' spear. The Veil's opening was on the west coast of the United States in California. She thought that was cruel, looking back on it now, but she must not have wanted it anywhere near her.

Once she and Frank returned, she saw a video of it. Or rather, she saw what the government had done to its door. It now had a massive circular dome built over it, and according to the federal government, they were figuring out how to let migrants come through in a safe and orderly fashion. So far, they hadn't figured it out, but Claire wasn't going to concern herself with it. She had set it up so that Earth could be friends with Mythers if they wanted, but she had no desire to get into the politics.

Frank ended up going off on her once they got back through, but Claire let it wash over her. She was glad to have him back, and he could yell or be as angry as he wanted. She knew it wouldn't last forever.

There was the debriefing with the FBI, but this time with people higher up than Remington or Lance. Jack and Marissa were there, too, although no one else was allowed in. Not the dean, not Byron, not even the FBI agents who had recruited everyone. All in all, it was a nerve-wracking interview, and the FBI seemed very concerned about the powers the three possessed.

Marissa's and Jack's had disappeared. Claire's? She didn't know, so she honestly couldn't tell the FBI anything. The one time she had for sure been able to use it, she'd been under great stress. Of the three, her power was the greatest, but it had almost killed her, and she had no interest in using it again.

Eventually, the FBI realized there wasn't a lot they could do. The three students were national heroes. International heroes, really. It wasn't like they could simply put them in a black site until they figured everything out.

A few months passed, and things started calming down.

After the media quit calling daily, and the FBI seemed to have no more questions, the dean invited a small group to her beach house in South Carolina. She called it a reunion as a joke, but it felt like one all the same. Byron, Jack, Marissa, and Claire all got invites, sent in the mail. Claire and Jack each got a plus one for theirs, although it was clear who they were supposed to invite. Jack would bring Sam, and Claire would bring Frank.

It hadn't been hard to convince the leprechaun to come, because the invitation had specifically said there would be unlimited alcohol for those of age.

The parents were invited to come as well, and Claire's treated it like the only vacation they'd had in over a decade —which it was.

It turned out to be a lot of fun. The dean's house was large, and it sat on a secluded part of the beach, with a pier that stretched out over the water.

Jack's eyes were wide when he saw it for the first time. "I guess working in academia pays pretty well, huh, Dean Pritcham?"

"I drove a pretty hard bargain with the FBI after everything was said and done. Called it hazard pay. This thing was on the market, so I went ahead and scooped it up."

Jack nodded and gave one of his grins. "I'm going to need hazard pay, too."

Remington and Lance ended up getting pretty drunk that night, with Lance finally putting a lampshade on his head before falling asleep on the couch. All in all, it was a good time, and while there was a lot of happiness, no one tried discussing the war. They all let it lie since there wasn't any reason to point it out. Leaving the topic alone felt right.

When the adults had finally fallen asleep, the former students walked down to the dock and sat down. The waves lapped against the wooden posts, and the moon shone across the ocean as it had every night for millions of years. They were all seated before they realized Dr. Byron was standing on the corner of the dock.

Marissa almost jumped out of her skin. "Goodness, Professor! Were you going to tell us you were here?"

Byron gave a small belch. He'd had a few drinks tonight as well. "You don't see the green one on the other side yet, do ye?"

Frank burped from the other corner of the dock, his much louder. "The professor is trying to steal me words. He doesn't sound as good, though."

Jack laughed as he took Sam's hand. Claire and Marissa laid back on the dock and stared up at the stars. "What were you two doing down here?" Claire asked. "We thought you'd both passed out."

Frank scoffed. "Pass out? Me? No chance. You humans might not be able to handle your liquor, but I'm a professional."

Marissa rolled her eyes. "They call that being an alcoholic, Frank."

The leprechaun shrugged. "To-may-toe, tah-mah-toe." He took another swig of his beer.

Byron crossed one leg over the other as he leaned against the railing. "Came down here to talk about everything that happened. There seemed to be an unspoken rule up there that no one would discuss it."

Jack laid down on the dock, too, Sam putting her head on his chest. "I'm just glad you all made it back," she said. "Talking about it feels? I don't know. Scary, I guess. Like it might all happen again somehow."

No one said anything for a few moments. Finally, Marissa turned her head so she was looking at the professor. "Do you think it's over? Or do you think Zeus might try something else?"

The professor studied the water for a few seconds before bringing his can of beer to his lips. He took a gentle sip and then brought it back down. "'Over' might be a very, very long time."

"What's that mean?" Marissa followed up.

The professor's eyes were distant as he stared out across the black water. "It means that it might not be over forever, but it could be over for now. I guess it means what Zeus told Claire. It's over for now, but he's not done with us."

Frank stepped away from the railing and walked over to the open area next to Marissa. He sat down, dangling his feet off the dock. "Are ye all worried about it?"

No one said anything for a few moments, and Claire knew she was meant to answer. In the end, she had been the one to stare down the gods and send them away. If the Veil tore again, the world would need Claire. "Yeah, I guess I am. I almost died the last time, and I wonder if I will be able to stand up to them again. Maybe my body won't be able to handle it. I'm not living in fear day in and day out, but I guess it's always in the background. What if Zeus tries again and I'm not up to the task?"

Frank finished his beer, and then placed the can on the

pier next to him. He slammed his hand down on it and flattened it, then picked it up and skipped it across the ocean. It went fifty feet out, skipping at least five times before it finally sank. "Ye know what I'm worried about? How much beer is up in that house. I'm worried about whether I'll be able to get me pot of gold back or at least find another one. Rainbows are few and far between over here.

"I'm worried about how the government is going to start treating the Mythers now that the immediate threat is gone. There's a lot to worry about in this world, I won't deny it." Frank laid down on the pier so that he was staring up like the other four. "I'll tell ye this, though. I'm not worried about Zeus or those other gods. It's not because of any powers ye all have now, either. Truth be told, I wasn't worried from the time I met Claire, and when the rest of ye jokers got involved, I knew we had it in the bag."

He sighed, then paused for a few moments.

"I guess what I'm trying to tell ye all is simple. I hope Zeus tries again because if he does, I'm going to enjoy livin' the remainder of me life on Mt. Olympus."

Claire smiled as she looked at the sky. She didn't know —couldn't know—what the future held, but she was sure of one thing. She'd be happy to face it with this group of friends.

The End

Thanks for finishing the series! I sincerely hope you enjoyed it. Amy and I are thinking about how we can further the universe, because we do think it really has potential for more stories. Hell, it's an unlimited universe, where anything the mind can dream up can literally take place. If that sounds like something you might be interested in, drop me a message at jacemitchellwriter@gmail.com.

So, writers make PLENTY of mistakes, and our editors – may a Higher Power bless them. In this book, when writing about the dragon, I was told that my original draft said, "He lowered his snout and sniffed the ground, as a bull would have done toward a maître-D'."

Everyone at LMBPN got a good laugh at that, but my argument was: technically I'm not wrong. Even if it wasn't what I meant to say. .

I got a good laugh at it, and I'm so glad our editors caught it before you all did.

Until next time,
Jace

SNAKES AND SHADOWS

If you enjoyed this book, you might also enjoy the Penny and Boots series from Amy Hopkins. Book one is *Snakes and Shadows* and it's available now!

Grab your copy today at Amazon or through Kindle Unlimited.

BOOKS BY JACE MITCHELL

Hand of Justice Series
The Dark Mage (1)
Chasing Magic (2)
Magic Rising (3)
Magic Unchained (4)

Paranormal University
Paranormal University: First Semester (1)
Paranormal University: Second Semester (2)
Paranormal University: Third Semester (3)
Paranormal University: Fourth Semester (4)

www.ingramcontent.com/pod-product-compliance
Lightning Source LLC
Chambersburg PA
CBHW050228110726
47898CB00007B/2072